"If I move in with you, then we can create a family unit that may not be like another person's but that works for us."

"One that has two people both wanting to do the best thing by the child," Ivan agreed hoarsely.

And she tried not to let her heart race away when he gazed down at her, a flicker of surprise and something else she couldn't quite decipher in his eyes.

"It will still be more than either of us ever got to experience," he continued. "A chance to break the cycle. For me, at least."

"Yes. Exactly."

It was meant to be a moment of clarity. Ruby knew that. But as their eyes locked, she felt something shift between them. Ivan's usually guarded expression softened, if only for a moment, and she caught a glimpse of that well-hidden vulnerability that made her heart ache.

Almost as though he didn't realize what he was doing, he slid his hands to her shoulders, moving her back slightly so he could look straight into her eyes...

Dear Reader,

I love the idea of Little Meadwood, with its river cottages, its village green, and Vivian—the foster mother who brought such light into the lives of so many.

When I first had the idea for a duet with Ruby and Ivan along with Nell and Connor, I knew that only one of the most life-changing events could pull Ruby and Ivan back together. An unexpected pregnancy! How could Ruby, having never left Little Meadwood, and Ivan, who had made a life for himself in the anonymity of a city like London, pull together to create a ready-made family for their imminent arrival, especially when Ivan had never really faced the horrors of his past or healed?

I knew that Ruby would have to be the one to finally break down his armor, but it turned out that her way of doing so differed from what I had originally envisaged for her.

I truly hope you enjoy reading Ruby and Ivan's story as much as I enjoyed writing it (or Ruby *telling* me how I ought to write it!).

I absolutely love hearing from my readers, so feel free to drop me a message at www.charlotte-hawkes.com or find me on Facebook or Instagram.

Charlotte x

NURSE'S BABY BOMBSHELL

CHARLOTTE HAWKES

Recycling programs for this product may not exist in your area.

ISBN-13: 978-1-335-94290-6

Nurse's Baby Bombshell

For questions and comments about the quality of this book, please contact us at CustomerService@Harlequin.com.

Harlequin Enterprises ULC
22 Adelaide St. West, 41st Floor
Toronto, Ontario M5H 4E3, Canada
www.Harlequin.com

Printed in U.S.A.

Born and raised on the Wirral Peninsula in England, **Charlotte Hawkes** is mom to two intrepid boys who love her to play building block games with them and who object loudly to the amount of time she spends on the computer. When she isn't writing—or building with blocks—she is company director for a small Anglo/French construction firm. Charlotte loves to hear from readers, and you can contact her at her website: charlotte-hawkes.com.

Books by Charlotte Hawkes

Harlequin Medical Romance

Billionaire Twin Surgeons

Forbidden Nights with the Surgeon
Shock Baby for the Doctor

Royal Christmas at Seattle General

The Bodyguard's Christmas Proposal

Reunited on the Front Line

Second Chance with His Army Doc

The Doctor's One Night to Remember
Reunited with His Long-Lost Nurse
Tempted by Her Convenient Husband
His Cinderella Houseguest
Neurosurgeon, Single Dad...Husband?
Trauma Doc to Redeem the Rebel

Visit the Author Profile page at Harlequin.com.

To Monty, Bart and Derek.

Fifty ducks, one hundred fish
and a thousand seagulls...

No, wait, that one's another duck!

Praise for
Charlotte Hawkes

"[The author's] research for this book is evident and lends a very authentic touch. With her talent, author Charlotte Hawkes could probably write in any sub-genre, but she brings this medical story to life."

—*Harlequin Junkie* on
Tempted by Her Convenient Husband

CHAPTER ONE

'RUBY CHANNING FOR Ivan Volkov, please.'

Summoning her brightest smile, and endeavouring to quash the kaleidoscope of butterflies that was currently performing aerobatics in her stomach, Ruby attempted to charm her way past the formidable receptionist in the prestigious Harley Street Clinic.

Clearly, however, her charm had failed if the weight of the woman's disapproving gaze was anything to go by; it was pressing down on Ruby as though about to squeeze the last bit of air from her lungs.

'*Dr* Volkov is very busy,' the receptionist corrected. Pointedly. 'Did you have an appointment, *Ms* Channing, is it?'

'Channing, yes,' Ruby confirmed, not sure how she was managing to keep her smile in place. As if the mere act of being here in the first instance wasn't enough to fill her with cold horror. As if she actually *wanted* to be here. 'And technically, *no,* I don't have an appointment but I'm sure he'll see me if he knows—'

'I'm afraid that is out of the question.' The woman cut her off with a tight, if professional, smile. 'Dr Volkov's appointment schedule is full. Several months in advance, in fact.'

Of course it was. Ruby could have kicked herself—possibly quite literally. She knew how busy Ivan was, how much of a career-driven, workaholic surgeon he was. He had fought to get an army scholarship to put himself through his medical degree at uni, honed his skills on the battlefield in numerous theatres of war, and had now become one of the foremost plastic surgeons to the stars.

It had always delighted Vivian, their former foster mother, every time he'd called her to see how she was, only for her to demand an update on his life. Not to mention the occasions—possibly once a year or so—that Ivan had actually driven back to Little Meadwood to see her.

As he should. Vivian had been the only real mother he'd ever known.

Ruby had often wondered if Ivan's work ethic was as much about making Vivian proud as it was about anything else that had happened in his childhood.

Not that she knew all that much about his past. It was something Ivan had never really discussed—not when she'd been his foster sister for all of five minutes those many years ago, nor in those fleeting reunion encounters over the decade and a half since, and certainly not in that unexpected, lust-fuelled weekend the two of them had shared fourteen weeks earlier.

Blinking back the X-rated memories that abruptly tried to crash their way into her thoughts, and pretending her skin didn't burn at the mere memory, Ruby fought to focus on the blank-faced receptionist in front of her. She cast around to try to remember the last thing the woman had said.

Ah...right... Ivan's appointment schedule was full.

With hindsight, it had been foolish to simply appear at his clinic as though she was simply dropping in off the street. As though coming here was an afterthought rather than the result of driving five hours, in the early hours of the morning, to try to catch Ivan at the beginning of his working day, just for this specific purpose. Even though there were a million other things Ruby would rather have to do than have this particular conversation with Ivan.

Still, she couldn't quite bring herself to leave either, as much as part of her welcomed the excuse to do precisely that. To be fair, if she walked away now then at least she could say that she'd tried. She'd attempted to talk to Ivan. She'd attempted to do the right thing.

Only that sounded lamentably inadequate. As though she'd just given up at the first hurdle. And this was too important for that. As unpalatable as the prospect of the conversation might be, she hadn't driven several hours to simply turn around and head back—defeated—to her home in the small rural town of Little Meadwood.

Maintaining her smile but adding a touch of self-deprecation, Ruby tried to sound suitably respectful.

'I appreciate how busy Dr Volkov is, of course.' She was careful not to use Ivan's first name this time. 'However, it really is important that I speak with him. Today.'

Still, it wasn't a surprise that the receptionist looked wholly unmoved.

'Indeed?' She didn't precisely raise her eyebrow, but the effect was much the same. 'Even so, Dr Volkov has back-to-back clinics with patients who have waited months for their appointments, and as you yourself have already acknowledged, you are most certainly not in the appointment book.'

'Really? Back-to-back clinics?' The words were tumbling out and Ruby was sweeping her arm around the empty waiting room before she could stop herself.

The receptionist pressed her lips into a thin, unimpressed line before continuing. 'The calibre of clinic, and patients, that Dr Volkov runs means patient discretion is taken very seriously here.'

'Of course.' Ruby nodded apologetically even before the other woman had finished speaking.

As a renowned plastic surgeon and a partner in a private clinic, Ivan carried out procedures for some of the richest and most famous, and they prized their privacy almost above all else. Having one patient bump into another in the waiting room would be more than a mere faux-pas—it could be career damaging.

'I sometimes forget how different it is this side of the fence,' Ruby continued, hoping she looked suitably remorseful. 'I work in the A&E department of a busy city hospital.'

'You didn't mention that before.' The receptionist blinked in surprise. 'Is this visit in relation to a patient?'

She may not have planned it, but it was the opening Ruby needed.

'In a sense.' Ruby nodded. 'I know you'll respect the sensitivity of the situation.'

'Of course' The receptionist narrowed her eyes as if trying to decide whether to believe Ruby or not.

Evidently she was going to have to offer at least a little more detail before the woman was satisfied.

'I'm sure you're aware that Dr Volkov spent a week away on a personal nature a few months ago…' Ruby tailed off, suspecting Ivan wouldn't have revealed too much about his trip back to Little Meadwood to visit his terminally ill former foster mother—much less that he would have mentioned their own far more personal encounter.

Her body burned again—even hotter this time—and Ruby began to despair of herself. If this was what mere memories did to her, she almost feared how she would react to actually being in the same room with Ivan again.

Almost.

'I understood that he had to visit family,' the receptionist said carefully, oblivious to the tremor that rippled through Ruby at the words.

'Family,' she echoed with a nod, her mouth suddenly dry. Vivian would be so proud to hear that Ivan described her that way. 'It was unavoidable.'

'Because of a serious illness,' the receptionist continued, trying to sound professional although Ruby suspected that deep down, she was desperate to know more.

'Right.' Ruby swallowed back the lump that had abruptly lodged itself in her throat. 'And now I think Ivan and I need to discuss a new situation that has arisen.'

The decision to revert to Ivan's first name was deliberate, and for the first time the receptionist hesitated, seeming less certain of herself. Even so, Ruby hated mentioning Vivian's diagnosis, especially when their former foster mother wasn't the reason she was here. But it was clear that there was no other way of getting past the receptionist.

And she felt sure Vivian would have approved. After all, hadn't her foster mother always taught her beloved foster kids that, since many of them had already had instilled in them the harsh reality that life could be unjust and cruel, they should always be prepared to think outside the box, especially when it came to people trying to deny them or exclude them?

‘I see.’ The receptionist looked put out. ‘You didn’t mention, when you came in, that your visit was in relation to a patient.’

‘I did not,’ Ruby agreed cheerfully, though her tone was more feigned than genuine. ‘My apologies. I was hoping to remain as tactful as possible. There is no change to the family member concerned, but I do need to discuss a matter that has subsequently arisen.’

‘This is highly irregular,’ the woman stated tightly.

‘As I said, I know Ivan will also appreciate your discretion,’ Ruby added hastily, this time summoning a cheerful but apologetic smile, refusing to feel guilty when the receptionist looked cornered.

‘I’ll speak with Dr Volkov but I can’t guarantee anything,’ the woman clipped out at last, tapping long fingernails on the keyboard as she weighed up her choices—which Ruby couldn’t help but suspect were more about impressing Ivan than wanting to do the best thing for the patient.

Another one of the man’s groupies, no doubt. Hardly a surprise—she was all too well acquainted with the kind of commotion Ivan made when he walked into a room. Even *before* he walked in. She’d seen it the weekend a few months earlier when she and Ivan, caught up in their unexpected shared memories of their former foster mother, had ended up going for a drink together to share old memories. Then another drink. Then a meal.

Ironic how watching women vie for adult Ivan's attention had somehow made her feel like a gawky teenager again, mooning after fifteen-year-old Ivan through the unfortunate fog of her schoolgirl crush.

For almost a year, each time her beloved birth mother had gone into hospital for treatment and she'd ended up back in Vivian's care, there had been a tiny, traitorous part of Ruby that had thrilled at the prospect of spending another weekend, week, or even month, under the same roof as the inescapably cool Ivan.

Not that he'd ever noticed her, treating her and her best friend, Nell—Vivian's other long-term foster child, who was still Ruby's best friend to this day—as little more than annoying kid sisters.

Except that Ivan hadn't looked at her like a kid sister on that brief visit a few months ago, had he?

Ruby shivered at the delicious memory of their last encounter. Even now, despite her determination to remain unaffected by the great Ivan Volkov, there was no denying that spark of electricity between the two of them that had been building on those fleeting visits these past couple of years. And this time, from the moment he'd walked through the door of Vivian's cottage, it had been so palpable to Ruby that she'd been shocked that neither her astute former foster mother nor her shrewd best friend had picked up on it.

Ruby shook her head sharply, as if to empty it of the unbidden memories. The last thing she needed was for her brain to be mobbed by spine-tingling, heart-pounding images of Ivan Volkov. Six foot three inches of sinfully chiselled muscle and wickedly handsome charm, hot and naked, and all hers.

She had to stay focused. There was no room in this scenario for personal feelings to cloud her judgement, especially since she'd finally plucked up the courage to come here in the first instance. Something she'd been vacillating over wildly for the past couple of weeks.

Not to mention the receptionist's stare, which continued to bore into her, seemingly searching for any sign of weakness or vulnerability.

And Ruby felt both. In spades. Even so she held her ground, maintaining her composed demeanour.

'I appreciate that it may seem irregular to you.' Ruby fought every urge to load those last two words with accusation. 'However, I know that Ivan will want to know what I've come to tell him.'

Well, she hoped he would, anyway.

Another long stare as the receptionist clearly grappled with Ruby's professional tone and her personal connection. Then, finally, the woman slipped into the glass office behind the reception area and picked up the phone, the conversation shielded from the luxurious waiting area.

It was all Ruby could do not to scan the woman's face for any signs of how the conversation was going. And as her heartbeat began to ramp up in her chest, she almost wished that Ivan would refuse to see her. At least she could say again that she had tried.

'Dr Volkov will see you,' the woman grated out at length, clearly disliking not knowing what was going on. She probably ran this place like the tightest of ships. 'But a word of warning, keep it brief as he is a very busy man.'

'Of course,' Ruby murmured softly.

There was no point in deliberately stirring up complications that could be avoided. Her life had enough inescapable perturbations in it right now as it was.

The receptionist bobbed her head, slightly mollified as she pressed the button to release some discreet lock on the door that led to the consultation rooms.

'Down the corridor, left at the end, and then it's the first room on the right.'

'Thank you.' Ruby nodded her thanks and made her way to the door.

But even as she walked down the corridor, each step felt heavier than the last. There were no words to describe quite how sick she felt. No stopping her legs from shaking ridiculously beneath her. Was it too late to turn around and flee?

Much too late, a voice remonstrated in her head, giving her a metaphorical shove down the corridor.

But within a few paces doubt gnawed at the edges of her fresh wave of resolve, threatening to unravel her already fragile composure. Her footsteps echoing on the marble floors didn't much help. What if she was making a mistake? What if Ivan *didn't* want to know what she had to say?

And it was all very well telling herself—for the umpteenth time—that it wouldn't matter, that at least she'd know she'd tried. But her conscience would still be there to needle her that she hadn't really tried very hard at all. The truth was that she knew all too well that something of this magnitude deserved at least a little more effort—and no matter that she would have given anything to be anywhere else but here, right in this moment.

For a second, Ruby slowed in the corridor. The sunlight filtered through a vast window that looked out onto a pretty garden she would expect to see back home in Little Meadwood rather than here, at a clinic in the middle of London.

Flowers bloomed blissfully in various glorious shades of pink and purple that were a stark contrast to the ugly streak of dark fear that seemed to be staining her from the inside out right now. The tranquillity of the space on the other side of the glass seemed to call to her, and before she realized it, she was turning slowly and stepping up to the pane, her forehead resting momentarily on the cool glass as though she might draw some strength from the serene scene beyond.

She had no idea how long she stayed like that, seeking solace in the comfort the view offered her. Perhaps it was a minute, perhaps an age. But it was only when Ivan's voice penetrated her thoughts that she sprang back, her head jerking around sharply.

'Ruby? What are you doing?'

Pushing herself slowly off the glass, Ruby turned to see where Ivan had appeared around the corner at the end of the corridor, and instantly her breath caught in her throat, her world kicking into gear and beginning to spin on its very axis.

Damn him to hell for the effect he always had on her.

Tall, imposing and undeservedly good-looking, the mere sight of him was enough to send fire licking through her veins. She hated how she noticed everything about him, from his ruffled hair, which was just a little longer than last time she'd seen him, to the impeccable Savile Row suit trousers and waistcoat he wore over the crispest of white shirts.

And she hated even more that not even a second in his presence and already her pulse kicked inside her. Hard. Stirring up that familiar, aching, yearning desire in her gut; building it up.

Ruby thrust it down savagely, berating herself for such a visceral reaction to the man after everything that had happened between them. She was not some schoolgirl with a crush anymore, but rather a grown woman who had more than held her own that passionate weekend they'd shared. The simple idea that she kept allowing Ivan to catapult her back to their teenage years together—where she had followed him around doe-eyed whilst he barely registered her existence—irritated her immensely.

Especially given the circumstances.

Lord, but how was she to even begin to discuss the…*circumstances*…with him?

'I was just admiring the garden.' She tried to summon a cheerful smile but it eluded her.

'What's wrong?' he asked as he started moving towards her. 'Has something happened to Vivian?'

'She's fine,' Ruby assured him hastily, despite her tumultuous emotions. 'At least, as well as can be expected. I did explain to your receptionist that there was no change.'

She couldn't bring herself to say any more. They both—along with all the many foster children who had returned to Little Meadwood to pay their respects in recent months—knew that Vivian's conditional was terminal.

Not that that stopped the indefatigable octogenarian from trying to care for her former charges rather than have them care for her.

'Indeed. But I wondered if you were simply trying to be discreet.'

'Right.' She nodded guiltily.

She *had* been trying to be discreet. But not for that reason.

She was almost relieved when he turned wordlessly and led the way to his consulting room, leaving her to follow. And she commanded herself to absolutely *not* notice his broad shoulders, which made her palms itch with the memory of running her hands over them.

Just as she would not consider how his short, dark hair seemed to catch the sunlight in a way that reminded her how soft it had been when she'd laced her fingers through it when his head had been buried, so deliciously sinfully, between her legs.

Without warning, Ruby let out a low grunt of frustration—at least, she told herself that it was frustration.

Ivan swung around instantly, and the familiar scent of his cologne wafted towards her and stirred up memories she had no business indulging. Certainly not with such a fervour.

'Sorry.' She feigned a cough. 'Must be the… dust.'

Except there wasn't a speck of dust in the place. It wouldn't dare. When Ivan Volkov commanded a place to be spotless, that was exactly what it was.

Squeezing her hands together so tightly that she could feel her fingernails digging painfully into her palms, Ruby instructed herself to start moving forward again and to compose herself. This nervousness wasn't her. She was usually so in control, and so capable under pressure, especially as a nurse who spent so much of her time calming panicking patients or their families.

But this was different. It wasn't usually *her* being affected by a situation. Which was probably why right now her nerves were a tangle of yarn in her stomach, and she feared that trying to unravel them would only pull at them and make them more of a mess than ever.

Wordlessly, she followed Ivan into the room, startled to discover that it wasn't so much a consultation room as his personal office.

Did that make this easier? Or harder?

Ruby bit her lip, trying to summon the courage to state what she'd travelled all this way to say.

'This definitely isn't about Vivian?' Ivan demanded; his low voice still tinged with concern.

Ruby shook her head emphatically. 'Not at all. I'm sorry for making you worry,' Ruby told him—and this, at least, was sincere. 'For the record, she's still fighting the diagnosis every step and pill of the way, of course.'

'I'd expect no less,' Ivan rumbled, looking momentarily relieved before sliding into the captain's chair behind a stunning-looking desk.

His very essence seemed to fill the space, commanding yet comforting all at once. The room was arranged with characteristic Ivan precision; medical texts lined the shelves, but the effect was somewhat softened by the choice of warm oaks and green baize linings that soothed the eye and somehow brought inside a touch of that verdant garden to which she had been so desperate to escape moments earlier.

Her gaze wandered for a while, flickering over everything and taking it all in until, eventually, it came to rest on Ivan himself. And on his dark gaze, which always seemed to have the power to skewer her.

'Why are you here, Ruby?'

It was the million-dollar question, wasn't it?

She took a moment to gather herself, folding her hands neatly in her lap if only to stop herself from fumbling with them.

Rip the Band-Aid off, her mother had always said—even when it was the news neither of them had wanted to discuss. Like another hospital visit. Another long course of debilitating treatment. She had never shied away from telling her daughter the truth about her illness. Never pretended she was going to get better when she knew it wasn't possible. But never let the fact that she was dying make their precious time together become negative.

Lost in her thoughts, Ruby was pulled back to the present by another growl from Ivan. A growl that made her think of other things…like those wickedly sinful sounds he had made that night a few months ago. When neither of them had been in control, yet both of them had decided control was an illusion. Especially when it had come to sending each other to the edge.

'I thought we agreed that what happened between us that night—' he began in a voice that sounded entirely too thick with memories.

And need. Even now.

'We did,' she cut him off hastily with a shake

of her head, not wanting to hear him dismiss their night together as a mistake or some such brush-off.

Especially not now.

'We did agree that,' she repeated, drawing in a steadying breath. 'And I was trying to respect that. But this is different.'

She was surprised at just how even and calm she sounded despite the emotions churning around inside her.

'Indeed?' Ivan frowned, the crease between his brows deepening as he tried to piece the puzzle together.

He leaned back in his chair but the seemingly casual gesture didn't fool her for an instant. The walls of the room might as well have been closing in on her; the tension was growing thicker with every passing moment, as if the two of them were the only two people left in the entire world.

Which only made it that much more apparent that she had no place left to hide, and no conversation left to throw into the space between them. She wasn't going to be able to escape the moment any longer. And so, finally, Ruby steeled her shoulders, met Ivan's too-intense stare head-on, and decided, *To hell with it.*

'The thing is, I'm pregnant.'

CHAPTER TWO

'PREGNANT?' IVAN REPEATED, rolling the word around his mouth as though tasting it.

Apparently, he didn't much like what he sampled. *Not,* Ruby commanded herself firmly, *that the act hurt her.*

Not one bit.

'Pregnant,' she confirmed. Cheerfully.

And no matter the storm inside her.

'I think not,' he concluded.

Still not hurt, decried the manic voice inside her head.

And any awkwardness she felt was mere apprehension rather than any lingering sexual tension. Which would, of course, be wholly inappropriate given the circumstances. She squared her shoulders and wondered how she was even managing to keep her voice level.

'Ah well, I'm afraid the test results say otherwise.'

His dark gaze skewered her to the spot.

'I fail to see how.'

'Really?' *Cheery, cheery, cheery.* 'As a surgeon, I would not have thought the basics of human reproduction would elude you.'

Ivan cast her the kind of withering look Ruby

was sure might intimidate any other woman, but somehow only lent her a sudden, much-needed boost of confidence.

Oddly, this was the Ivan she recognized best. The distant, guarded Ivan—not the passionate, seductive Ivan of the other month. *This,* she could deal with.

'I've no doubt your glowers work on others, Ivan Volkov.' She ran her hands down the front of her jeans with feigned nonchalance. 'You might be a top surgeon—not to mention something of a war hero, by all accounts—but you forget I knew you when you were that teen rebel. I remember all too well Vivian sitting us all around that tiny table of hers, laying down the house rules as she baked us cookies and made us hot chocolate with marshmallows.'

For a moment, Ivan almost smiled at the unexpected memory. But then his gaze dropped to her waist.

'My point is that we only had… We used protection.'

'That's true,' she acknowledged as he plunged on.

'Therefore, I can only conclude that there must be some mistake.'

And his tone held a finality as though there was nothing left to be said about the situation.

It seemed the man before her hadn't changed all that much from the hurt, angry boy who had always sworn he would never, *never* bring a child into the world. He'd always been adamant that no kid would ever endure the cruel upbringing that he had endured.

Not that he'd ever really talked about his years with his bully of a father. Not in any depth. But he hadn't needed to. Growing up with a single mother who had been in and out of hospital for years, Ruby had seen enough other foster homes to know that Ivan's terrible story was lamentably all too familiar.

How many times had she and Nell given silent thanks that their own childhoods, whilst filled with loss, had also been full of love?

Nell's parents had clearly adored their only child right up until their fatal car accident had robbed them of each other. Just like her own loving mother, who had always made Ruby feel like the most loved kid who existed, and every time Annabel Channing had gone into hospital for more treatment, or another operation, Ruby had known she'd done so because she was fighting her illness just to have another week, month, year, with her beloved daughter.

Without warning, Ruby's eyes prickled at the memory.

How she missed her mother. Especially now—expecting a child of her own. The need to hear her mother's voice just one more time, just for one more golden nugget of advice—or even just to hear Annabel tell her how much she loved her—was almost overwhelming.

Losing her loving, determined mother had been

more pain than the young Ruby had ever thought she could bear. She was only so very fortunate that Vivian had always been the most incredible foster mother. But that only made Vivian's terminal diagnosis all the more potent.

Just as it made this unborn baby all the more precious, Ruby realized with a jolt. She had to give this tiny being that was growing inside her all the love that both her mother and Vivian would have unarguably showered on such a wanted child.

Ruby blinked again, even more determinedly, as she amazed herself at her own show of calmness. Outwardly, at least.

'There's no mistake, Ivan,' she confirmed quietly but firmly. 'I *am* pregnant.'

Ivan glowered at her, even more appalled. Though for a shocking few moments, words seemed to fail him.

'No,' he rasped at length. 'I simply will not accept that.'

She almost laughed despite the fact she was shaking inside.

'Whilst I appreciate that you are able to bend many things to your will these days, even you cannot erase actual facts out of existence simply by willing them to be so.'

Ivan raised an eyebrow, those black eyes boring into hers with even more intensity than ever, and any sense of amusement dissipated. Something shifted inside her. What was it about the man that suddenly seemed almost…dangerous?

At least, dangerous to her heart, which was worse than anything else.

'You're saying the protection failed?'

'You're suggesting there is any other explanation?' she challenged. 'You think I did it deliberately?'

To his credit, Ivan met her gaze directly. 'No,' he confirmed. 'I do not believe that.'

'That's reassuring to hear.' She blew out a deep, steadying breath. 'And you aren't about to be completely disgusting and suggest that you think anyone else could possibly be the father? Or that you would actually think I would do something as amoral as to try to pass another man's child off on you?'

Because if he thought that little of her, then what hope did they even have of salvaging something… *civil*…out of this mess?

The look Ivan cast her was one of undisguised affrontery. If she'd thought he was mad at her before, it was nothing compared to the lethal glint in his eyes at that moment.

'That,' he bit out, as if the words were being ripped from his mouth, 'is not something I believe.'

And Ruby told herself that she didn't know why that should send such a wave of relief cascading through her.

* * *

The acknowledgement was out of Ivan's mouth almost before he had fully registered the implication.

He stood frozen; time seemed to come to a standstill around him as he struggled to process the magnitude of it. Even though they had used protection, there wasn't a single cell of him that believed Ruby would ever lie—which meant only one thing.

She was indeed pregnant, and he was the father.

The ticking clock on the wall of his office seemed to reverberate too loudly around the room, though the hands appeared stuck in the same position. He couldn't move, couldn't breathe.

He sure as hell didn't know what to think.

Was it only moments ago that he'd been staring down the corridor and wondering if her turning up at his clinic was real, or just another of the feverish dreams he'd been having almost every night since the one they'd spent together a few months earlier?

As if she'd been haunting his brain—and his body—ever since.

And then she folded her arms across her chest and tipped her head to the side, and the action was so familiar, so quintessentially Ruby, with that lashing of sass and that touch of defiance, that it hit him like a physical blow to the gut.

This was no ghost.

Memories flooded back—those late nights they'd spent a few months earlier, talking, reminiscing and laughing at the inside jokes that only they would have understood. And then, that final night they'd spent together, engaged in something far more intimate than mere shared memories of a long-forgotten past.

And still, as if against his will, he found his gaze sweeping slowly, appreciatively, over her. From that silky smooth caramel-brown hair that had poured through his fingers like the smoothest of water to that wickedly hot mouth that had done such things to him over and over again.

And from those mesmerizing hazel eyes that seemed to have possessed a direct line to her very soul, to the exquisite curves of body that had fit against his like two pieces of a puzzle that had been designed perfectly for each other. Was she as molten now as she had been that night?

What was he even thinking?

Sharply, Ivan pulled up the reins on his runaway brain. His body was responding to its own memories that his mind was fighting valiantly against replaying.

It wasn't as though he was a monk—far from it, despite his workaholic lifestyle—but when had any woman made him forget himself in such a primordial way?

The answer was simple—*never*—at least aside from little Ruby Channing. Or perhaps more accurately, the spellbinding woman she had grown into. Enough to make him lose his head.

Something snagged at Ivan's thought just then.

Quite *how much* had she made him lose his head a few months ago?

Enough to forget about something as fundamental as protection?

Now he thought about it—or at least, thought about it in cool, analytical terms rather than being assailed by the kind of feverish dreams that he had pretended hadn't haunted him almost every night since—it occurred to him that they'd both almost been too caught up in that first time together to remember whether they'd used protection.

The realization brought Ivan up cold. For a moment, he floundered, trying to work out what powerful sensation was bombarding him now.

He wanted to say he was in disbelief but what he felt was far, far more complex. *Him, a father.* He, who had always sworn from the age of six—or perhaps even earlier—that he would never, *never* continue the tainted, cruel, harsh Volkov bloodline.

And now Ruby was pregnant with his child.

Guilt, fear, uncertainty…they all swirled within him. Slowly at first, but then faster, harder, beginning to reverberate within him, making him feel as though he might throw up.

And then *crash.* They collided like turbulent waves in a stormy sea, making him feel more smashed apart than any shipwreck.

He had to stop it.

He *had* to.

But every way his brain turned—spinning this

way, then that—it seemed to hit a brick wall. And amid this maelstrom of emotions, Ivan felt something else stir within him.

Anger. At himself more than at Ruby, but unmistakable nonetheless. For giving in to temptation in the first instance that crazy night. For being so uncharacteristically carried away with Ruby that he had forgotten to be as fastidious about protection as he usually was. But also for the fact that when he'd stepped around that corner and seen Ruby standing there in his clinic, in *his* corridor, it had taken every ounce of willpower he'd had not to stalk up that corridor, haul her into his arms, and glut himself on this insane attraction that seemed to vibrate so frenetically between them.

Which was clearly how he'd got into this nightmare situation.

Pregnant.

No, he couldn't possibly become a father. What would he even know about raising a kid—certainly not how to raise a happy, healthy, undamaged kid?

Him, a father? Ivan wasn't sure how he didn't sneer aloud at the very title. His own had been a man who had only ever been a father by name but never by deed.

Too many of his foster fathers had been every bit as bad. And those few who might have shown a wild kid like him even a hint of kindness had soon seen the rotten streak that was imprinted through his core like a dropped apple, and soon insisted he be removed from their cosy homes.

Only Vivian had ever thought she could see something beyond his past. She was the kindest, fiercest, most generous foster mother he had never dreamed he might deserve.

Ironic that her unfailing love had only heightened his own sense of guilt that much more. Because even if he finally had someone like Vivian to care for him, and look out for him, then he'd only gained what he'd stolen from Maksim.

Instantly, Ivan stamped the thought out. Vehemently. He had no desire at all to gaze down that particular path into the past. Not even to let that name pass through his brain.

The pain and loss simply went too deep.

Even so, he had no idea how long he stood there, caught up in turbulent thoughts, until a soft cough from across the room tore him mercifully out of the maelstrom.

'Ivan?' Her hazel eyes were full of apprehension. 'Did you hear me?'

'I heard you,' he managed, his voice sounding foreign even to himself as he tried to guess what she might have been saying.

'Well, that's a start.' Ruby's voice sounded calm enough, but he didn't miss the shake in her too-tight smile.

As though she didn't quite believe him.

'Ruby…' Ivan began before stopping abruptly,

whatever he'd been about to say sticking in his throat like a dry pill.

But before he could cough the words out, he was startled by the sound of his name being called from out in the corridor, along with the fast *click-click* of stilettoes coming down the polished-stone hallway. Was it relief or instinct that had him darting across the room to spring open the door and step out into the open corridor beyond?

'It's an emergency.' His receptionist was pointing urgently back up the corridor. 'Someone has collapsed outside in the street. We don't think they are breathing.'

Ivan didn't need to hear any more. He was already halfway up the corridor before the receptionist had even turned around. Racing through the waiting area and into the crisp afternoon air as he took the steps two at a time down from his clinic to the street below, it was only when he reached the patient—blue faced and foaming at the mouth—that he realized Ruby was right there with him.

Dropping to his knees, he checked the motionless man. His mind somehow managed the shift from the whirlwind of emotions he'd been experiencing only moments earlier to the critical situation now at hand.

Though, for perhaps the first time, it wasn't as natural and easy to do.

'He isn't breathing,' Ivan confirmed to Ruby. 'I'll

start chest compressions. You need to grab the defibrillator from reception.'

Then he dropped his head to concentrate on what was in front of him, throwing himself into the task yet somehow not even needing to watch Ruby to know that she would be doing exactly as he'd asked with enviable efficiency.

Later, much later, well after this moment had passed, he would reflect on why he had found it so effortless to trust Ruby. And though he would tell himself it was just the result of having known her, on and off, for the better part of two decades, a part of him would know deep down that there was more to it than that.

But in that moment, Ivan's thoughts did not wander but were instead consumed with the urgency of the situation and the relief that Ruby was already back with the defibrillator. With a brief word of assurance to him that the receptionist was already calling 999, she began setting up the machine and running through the initial checks. Meanwhile Ivan focused on quickly unzipping his patient's top and pulling open the man's shirt in preparation for the AED.

'Charging to two hundred,' Ruby confirmed after a few moments. 'And clear.'

Sitting back, Ivan watched as Ruby delivered the first shock.

But there was no response from the unconscious

man, and a pulse check confirmed to Ivan that they needed to continue their efforts.

'Charge it again,' Ivan instructed as he bent back over to continue with CPR.

Not, it seemed, that he needed to. Ruby had already seamlessly begun to transition into the next cycle of defibrillation. As they worked in tandem, the intermittent blips and beeps from the machine was the only sound to punctuate the air.

'Okay,' Ruby said clearly but quietly after a moment. 'Clear.'

Instantly, Ivan straightened back up and removed all contact from the man.

A second shock. A second pulse check. And still, nothing.

'Charge it again,' Ivan commanded, dropping back to his exhausting task.

And as he and Ruby worked together for a third time, seemingly in harmony without even having to say more than a word here or there, the third and final shock was delivered. This time the man twitched.

'We have a pulse,' Ivan finally gritted out, just as the faint sound of an approaching ambulance could be heard in the distance. 'Good work.'

'And you.' Ruby nodded briefly.

Her focus, like his, was still primarily on the patient and for the next few minutes, they continued to work together in silent unison as they tried to keep their patient comfortable and ready for transport. By the time the paramedics were on scene, the now-breathing man was already waiting to simply be loaded onto the ambulance and taken straight to hospital. Ivan offered a concise, efficient handover and then it was done, and he found himself heading back inside his clinic with Ruby.

'That was good work back there,' he managed gruffly as they mounted the steps together.

'I could say the same. We made a good team.' Ruby's cheeks flushed in her haste to explain herself. 'I didn't mean…'

Her rich, hazel eyes met his and Ivan couldn't help feeling an unspoken sense of accomplishment. Every minute had counted with that man, and Ruby was right that together the two of them had saved a life through seamless teamwork. The image of her by his side, anticipating yet simultaneously being proactive, lingered in his mind. It inevitably made him wonder what else they might be able to achieve if they pulled together in a similar way.

Like raising a baby.

But the thought was no sooner there than it was gone again. Or, more accurately, Ivan was dismissing it.

The adrenalin from their successful resuscitation was already ebbing away, leaving the stark reality in its place. Being a surgeon who was capable of saving a life on the street was hardly the same thing as being a damaged human capable of raising a tiny human being without passing on that damage.

The weight of responsibility squatted in his chest, heavier than ever.

This—medicine, surgery—was what he was good at. Perhaps the only thing he was good at.

Being a decent human being, one capable of something as complex and impactful as *love...?* Well, that was something altogether different.

No matter how much he despised himself for it, it wouldn't make it any the less true. The sooner he could make Ruby realize it, the better for her.

'Reading too much into it is a mistake,' he bit out gruffly. Though whether he was talking to Ruby or himself wasn't entirely clear to him.

Stepping out of the corridor, he ushered her back into his office as she turned to glance at him over her shoulder just the way she had done several months earlier in her cottage doorway the night he had made the mistake of giving in to temptation.

'I was just saying—'

'I know what you were saying,' he cut her off, hating the way his body was reacting despite his brain telling him not to. 'And *I'm* just saying that the two things are mutually exclusive.'

'You really don't want anything to do with this baby?' Her voice cracked despite her obvious efforts not to let it whilst her hand moved instinctively to her stomach as if to protect the growing embryo inside.

'That isn't what I'm saying,' he rasped out instinctively before stopping himself.

What *was* he saying? He couldn't even work it out himself, which only made him feel even more of a deadbeat. It wasn't even a fetus yet, and he was already turning into a sorry excuse for a father. Just as he'd always feared.

Not that the realization should come as such a shock to him.

Had he really thought he was capable of anything better? No matter how much he wanted to be different from that cruel drunkard who had been his own father—and no matter how many long, long hours he had fought to make a success of his life—deep down, he couldn't change who he really was.

He wouldn't be any better a father than his own had been. It was how he was built, and no amount of hate and mental excoriation could ever hope to change it. The same tainted blood ran through his veins. The same distorted codes of DNA.

And he'd never hated himself more for it.

'Ivan, I understand that this is a lot to take in,' Ruby pressed on when he still didn't speak. 'It was for me when I first realized I was pregnant. But together…'

'There is no *together*, Ruby,' he heard himself grit out, though every word felt like glass in his mouth, mercilessly grinding at the soft, weak tissue. 'This cannot be. I will not accept it.'

And he steeled himself against the hurt that flashed across her gloriously expressive eyes.

He was acting for the best.

'Ivan, please…' She stepped forward unexpectedly, reaching for his arm.

'Stop!' He recoiled instantly, doing nothing to mask his horror, hating himself for the wounded expression that scudded across her lovely features.

But he couldn't back down. She didn't need to know that he wasn't so much appalled at the thought of her touch so much as at the way his skin crackled in hedonistic expectation.

As if he exerted no control whatsoever on what his body might want even now.

Especially now.

How could he possibly raise a child of his own with all that coiled inside him? Just waiting to strike. Just watching for the moment he let his guard down. He knew first-hand how destructive a bad parent could be. He knew exactly the damage such a man could do. What kind of an example would he be for any child?

It wasn't fair to them. Or to Ruby. They deserved better than him. They deserved better. Full stop.

'Having a baby with me is a terrible idea.' The words tumbled out of his mouth. 'More than that, it is unacceptable.'

She sucked in a sharp breath.

'Are you saying you want me to…not have this baby?'

Ivan startled. Something dark and sickening thudding through him. No matter what else he thought, that wasn't what he had said. And it sure as hell wasn't what he meant.

God, he was so damaged he couldn't even get this bit right.

Taking a moment to steady himself, Ivan tried sucking in a breath. But his lungs might as well have been on fire. His head was swimming. Churning. And with it, an anchor dragging him down into an abyss.

Surely all he'd meant was that no child deserved to be cursed with the Volkov bloodline?

He opened his mouth to explain, but the right words seemed to elude him.

Ruby, it seemed, wasn't having the same problem at all.

'Because that isn't happening,' she proclaimed emphatically. And if he noticed a slight edge of hysteria to her tone then, he certainly wasn't in a position to point it out. 'I *am* having this baby, Ivan.'

'No...' He worked his mouth, trying to loosen the suddenly stiff jaw and tongue. 'I can't...*won't* be a part of it.'

And he loathed himself that little bit more for that shimmer in her captivating eyes. The pain that he was patently causing.

Because that was all he was capable of doing.

'Fine,' she whispered, nodding her head jerkily. 'I only needed to know if you wanted to be a part of this. You don't, and that is your right. I'm not asking for anything from you.'

'You don't want anything from me?' he echoed instead, his jaw clenched so tight that the pain cascaded through him. 'I find that hard to believe.'

He refused to hear her gasp of shock. Or acknowledge that shimmer in her eyes.

'You can't really think that,' she managed. And he told himself he didn't hear any pain in her tone. 'I don't understand what's happening. This… It isn't you.'

He wasn't sure if what frightened him more was the thought that she was right or that she was wrong. But right now, he had found a rope and—whether it was a lifeline or a noose—it was all he had to cling to in that moment.

'You don't know the first thing about me.'

'I think I know you better than most,' she shot back.

'A few weeks here and there, in the same foster home, a couple of decades ago does not mean you know me.'

She actually arched her eyebrows at him, angrier than he had ever seen her. Though to be fair the Ruby he had known, however briefly, had never had much of a temper. She'd been more of a sulker; the memory popped unbidden into his head.

He shoved it aside, but she was already speaking.

'I know you were a guarded kid who had suffered a lot being shunted in and out of different foster homes and boys' homes, before you ended up at Vivian's.'

As if that even covered the half of what he'd been through.

The truth was enough to knock the air out of his lungs—just as his father had done over and over again from as young as Ivan could remember.

He spun away, no more able to face Ruby than he was able to face the memories of his father's cruelty. The countless nights and days spent cowering in his room in fear whilst his father raged at who knew what, too afraid to risk creeping down the stairs in a bid to escape. How many times had he shoved his little brother, Maksim, into the safety of the wardrobe, just in case their father burst in, looking for something or someone on whom he could take out his fury?

It had to have been thousands, over the years.

This time Ivan punched the memory away viciously, quickly, before the hazy edges of it sharpened and reminded him of even more details of the life he'd fooled himself that he'd left behind.

But beneath the troubled surface, her gaze held a steely resolve he had never been sure she'd appreciated she possessed.

If this baby was to stand a chance at a normal, toxic-free childhood, then Ivan was instantly convinced that Ruby Channing would be the person able to provide it. She was her own person, but with a healthy dose of their former foster mother thrown in for good measure.

As long as she stayed far away from him.

Which meant that however hard it was, he had to get Ruby to see that for herself.

'This baby—any baby—would be better off far away from me.'

'Fine…but I'm keeping it.' She took a step back, her eyes glistening with unshed tears. Yet she held herself together in a way that he could only admire.

'I would ruin it.'

Her chin lifted with a determination that transcended the apparent fragility of her emotions. It all made his chest ache with conflicting emotions that he couldn't even begin to comprehend.

'Whether you want to be involved or not is entirely up to you.'

Words raced around his head, and to the tip of his tongue, but Ivan couldn't quite grasp any of them properly. They were too slippery. Too fast. Even as Ruby turned her back on him, straightened her crease-free clothes, and finally lurched for the door.

And he should have let her go—just as he'd wanted her to do. But something made him call out to stop her.

'Ruby…'

She paused and turned, but that moment of weakness was over and Ivan was already regaining control of himself. He didn't continue, telling himself that he had no idea what he'd even been going to say anyway.

'At least you know now,' Ruby eventually spoke

for him. Stiffly. Determinedly. 'You can't ever say that I didn't tell you.'

'You told me,' he echoed mechanically.

Unable to move. Numb. Though every part of his being was screaming at him.

Then Ruby reached for the door.

'Goodbye, Ivan.'

In the moment of silence that followed, a thousand, million thoughts slammed through his brain but he couldn't understand a single one of them.

And then she was hauling open the door and stepping outside, and all he could do was watch her go.

CHAPTER THREE

It was several hours—and multiple motorway stops for water, hot chocolate and anything else that might prevent her body from involuntarily shaking—by the time Ruby arrived back at Little Meadwood. And still nothing had quite settled her jangling nerves after her encounter with Ivan.

How could he have been so heartless? So utterly cruel?

She'd known that as a foster teen he'd been anti-family, but she'd assumed he would have changed with age. It had never occurred to her that he would want nothing—*nothing*—to do with their baby. And all right, so perhaps logic whispered that she might have been a little naive to think that it would go smoothly. After all, what self-respecting bachelor would be delighted to hear that a one-night stand had resulted in a pregnancy? But right now it wasn't her head that was firing emotions all through her body, but rather her aching heart.

Surely he hadn't needed to be quite so callous in his rejection? It wasn't as if they were complete strangers and he didn't know what her angle was. He *knew* her, well enough to know that she would never have deliberately engineered this situation anyway.

Right?

Thoughts ricocheted around her head, sending her lurching this way and that.

Admittedly, her foolish fantasy of cottage gardens and white picket fences that lurked at the back of her mind was probably a little fairy-tale laughable, but it hurt for him not to want to be any part at all of their unborn baby's life.

And as for any suggestion that she should not continue with the pregnancy…well, that stung far deeper than she could have imagined.

Except that he hadn't said that, had he? a tiny, muffled voice pointed out from the back of her head. He'd merely ascertained what she herself wanted to do, and then he had accepted it.

But she wasn't quite prepared to listen to such a voice of reason. Not when the events of the afternoon were still playing out wildly in her head, over and over, as if she could somehow make more sense of them.

She'd anticipated his shock. Even some degree of disbelief. But what hadn't occurred to her was that he would want nothing to do with this little life.

Her eyes prickled before she could stop herself; her hand moved instinctively, as it seemed to have a habit of doing these days, to cradle the nonexistent bump. As though she could somehow protect it from anyone who might want to hurt it.

She just hadn't expected that person would be Ivan.

A rush of what could only be described as *love* coursed through her in that moment.

She was going to have a baby!

As unplanned and terrifying as that prospect was, a part of her was thrilled. If she could be even half as generous and funny and strong as her own mother had been, then surely this baby could want for nothing.

She would make sure she was enough. More than enough.

Except it didn't work that way, did it? Something unpleasant snapped around her chest, making her struggle to breathe for a moment.

Because as loving and amazing as Annabel Channing had been, Ruby thought, she'd still lost her. Horribly. Because cancer didn't just hit once; it hit over and over, levelling not only its target but everyone else in its wake, too.

So how was she to explain to him or her, eight or ten years from now, why they didn't have a father? She didn't even know how she was to begin tackling that situation. After all, hadn't she wondered about her own father despite everything her mother had ever done for her?

And hadn't she been frustrated by her mother's evasiveness every time the topic had come up, hurt by the fact that she had never known even the slightest thing about the man who was her biological father?

There was a sense of a missing piece that she had

always sworn to herself she would never inflict on any baby of her own. Yet here she was repeating, it seemed, the same mistake. And there was nothing she could do about it.

Until this moment, she didn't think she had fully understood her mother's reasons for refusing to answer even a single one of her many questions.

But now, suddenly, it was all too clear.

'I promise you, little one,' Ruby whispered to her belly, 'that I will never, *never* let you feel you weren't always wanted.'

Even if that meant refusing to answer a single question about Ivan Volkov.

She stabbed her key into the lock of the small cottage she shared with her best friend and former foster sibling, Nell. Ruby didn't even attempt to unravel her hurt from her anger as she stumbled through the door, grateful to be home at last.

Then she stopped abruptly in the short, narrow hallway. She couldn't pinpoint it, but something felt somehow…*odd.*

'Nell?' she called out hesitantly, though she was sure her friend was supposed to be on duty at City Hospital, where they both worked.

Or could it just be that she was hoping her best friend would be here? Nell would listen to her, hug her, and make her laugh. And now that she'd told Ivan about the baby—for all the good it had done—it would be a relief to finally be able to share the news with her best friend. And with Vivian, for that matter.

'Not Nell,' a deep, familiar voice carried from the living room of the otherwise-still cottage.

A shiver of indignation rippled down Ruby's spine moments before Ivan's shadow filled the small doorway that led off the short hallway.

At least she told herself that it was indignation—certainly not anticipation—given that this was the man who was the very cause of her anguish. And so, in that moment, she levelled all her frustration and ire down the hall towards him.

'What are you doing here, Ivan? And who the hell let you into my home?'

He didn't appear to move even a muscle yet the controlled fury rolled out of him. Just like thunder. And she felt it rumbling around her, making all the tiny hairs on her arms rise up and setting of mini-jolts of lightning right through her body.

Of fury, she told herself firmly.

'Did you really think you could drop a bombshell like that and simply walk away from me?'

And she despaired of herself that her heart leaped like that, despite her own anger. But that didn't mean she had to give in to it.

'I didn't "drop a bombshell" then "walk away",' she heard herself answer. Tartly. 'I gave you the chance to discuss it and you made it clear you wanted nothing to do with me—with it. So I left. I didn't expect to walk through my own front door to find you'd broken in.'

Ivan's jaw tightened.

'I've hardly broken in. I used the spare key. Or have you conveniently forgotten that you were the one who showed me where it was hidden last time I was here?'

'I didn't forget.' She wrinkled her nose, begrudging the fact that she had to admit it.

She'd only shown him where the key was in case he needed somewhere to wait if he turned up to visit Vivian next door, only to find that she was asleep. Sometimes the treatment took it out of her.

No other reason. Certainly not that he could let himself in when all she'd wanted to do was get home, get a hot shower, and sink into her bed for what felt like a week's worth of sleep. She was exceptionally tired after her very early start this morning and hours of driving.

'I think we said all that we needed to say back in London, don't you?' she managed instead, proud of herself when her voice didn't shake or otherwise betray her.

Then told herself that she didn't feel anything somersaulting inside her when Ivan glowered at her like a winter storm ready to unleash itself.

'Not by a long way,' he growled, his voice low and dangerous.

A wiser woman might have taken heed but Ruby had never been wise where Ivan was concerned—

clearly—and she wasn't about to back down. Especially now when heat prickled at the back of her eyes and emotions bubbled up in her, threatening to spill over at any moment.

'Well, I've said all I needed to say,' she bit out at length.

'Good, then it will make this conversation short and sweet,' Ivan growled. 'In answer to your earlier question, I'm here to bring you home.'

Whatever she'd been expecting him to say, it hadn't been that.

'I *am* home.' She frowned, confused.

'I think not.'

A prickle of unease crept down her spine, like long, thorny fingers walking their way over each and every vertebra.

'Ivan…'

'You are expecting my child, Ruby.' He didn't shout, didn't even raise his voice, yet the sound seemed to echo deafeningly, off every wall in the cottage. 'Did you really think I would just let you raise it without me?'

Ruby had no idea how she managed to face him down.

'After what you said a few hours ago,' she managed defiantly, 'I had thought that was exactly what had been decided.'

At least he had the decency to look guilty at that. If only for a fraction of a second. Then he caught himself.

'Decided?' he echoed incredulously. 'You came in, dropped your bombshell, and then walked out.'

Indignation, and something else that Ruby didn't care to name, coursed through her.

'That isn't what happened. I…told you so you could choose whether to be involved or not. You chose the latter—'

'I had no chance to choose anything,' Ivan cut her off harshly. 'So now your only choice will be to move in with me.'

Did the world speed up, or slow down? Ruby couldn't tell. Her mind was too busy racing to catch up with the sudden turn conversation.

'Move in…with you?' she echoed, her breath more ragged than she would have liked. But that couldn't be helped. 'You cannot be serious.'

'I assure you I am perfectly serious.'

'But…' She floundered, her brain still lagging embarrassingly behind. 'How would that even work? I live here. I work at City Hospital. You live in London and you have a private practice.'

'Which is why it makes more sense for you to move in with me.'

Ruby gasped—the air almost choking her as surely as if she was caught in the crushing grip of the fiercest storm. This wasn't how she'd imagined her future. And yet…

She shook any traitorous thoughts out of her head.

'No.' The word shot out of her mouth like a crack from a gun. 'My job is here. My friends. My family.'

'Your mother was your only family, was she not?' Ivan frowned, clearly not trying to hurt her—merely being factual. 'Vivian fostered you because when she passed, you had no one else.'

'Vivian *is* my family,' Ruby bit out. 'And Nell. And everyone at Little Meadwood.'

There was no mistaking the exasperation in his expression but that was likely to be expected. Ivan might care for Vivian, but he had never seen Little Meadwood as a home. Certainly not the way she or Nell had done.

Little wonder that he had set up a new life in London, where he could be anonymous. Her heart ached for him.

'You could take a leave of absence. Or you could easily transfer to a London hospital.'

'My whole *life* is here, Ivan. I'm not leaving.'

'Not even for this baby for whom you profess to want to do what is best?'

The cottage walls seemed to press in closer, as if peering in to witness such a moment, and Ruby's hand trembled slightly as she reached up to tuck a loose strand of her brown hair behind an ear, her hazel eyes darting away from Ivan's piercing gaze. The silence in the cottage was thick, punctuated only by the quiet ticking of the old grandfather clock in the corner.

'Look, Ivan,' she began, her voice steadier than she felt given how heavy the words were on her tongue. 'I understand what you're saying, but we don't need to live together to raise this child. We don't have to be a couple.'

No matter that a traitorous part of her had wanted him to do just that.

But because he *wanted* to, not because of duty. How naive was that?

The pain of her own upbringing echoed through her plea. Despite the unconditional love of her mother, the absence of a father figure growing up had left her longing for completeness. Was that why the sting of Ivan's initial rejection at the clinic remained fresh—a wound that no amount of goodwill could easily soothe?

'No, we don't need to be a couple,' he agreed, his voice a low rumble that seemed to fill the room. 'But if we want to provide a stable home for our child, then perhaps it is the best option.'

He stepped closer, and the air around them seemed to shift suddenly, becoming charged with an intensity that Ruby hadn't anticipated.

'I'm not sure that *stable* means throwing together two people who barely know each other,' she countered, trying to ignore the way her heart hammered against her ribcage. 'And contrary to what I said before, growing up as foster kids in the same house twenty years ago doesn't count.'

So why was it that whilst the rational part of her brain screamed for distance—for protection against further hurt—some irrational part craved the connection he offered?

'So, let me get this straight,' Ivan ground out. Furious sparks actually seemed to spit out from his coal-black eyes. 'You travelled to London expecting me to leap at the chance to get to know a baby that I didn't even know existed until a few hours ago. Then you ran away when I didn't do precisely that. And now, when I say I will take responsibility, you claim we barely know each other.'

When he put it like that, it sounded nonsensical. But Ruby stood her ground.

'The fact is that you're only here now out of a sense of duty.'

'And you find that a problem?' he challenged, his voice edgier than she had ever heard him. 'What did you expect me to do, Ruby? Perhaps you thought I should throw a baby shower?'

'Obviously not,' she snapped again.

Which hardly helped to defuse the situation, but she found it impossible to do anything else.

'Then what?' His voice still echoed loudly in the small space.

Ruby wrinkled her nose but didn't answer. She didn't think he was looking for a response anyway. His eyes were too dark, and too intense, as they bored into her. The air was charged with electricity.

'Well?' he pushed, after a moment. 'I hurt you, I understand that. But you hardly gave me chance to do anything else.'

There was another beat of silence.

'I don't know what I expected.' She threw her hands up angrily. 'Just not...*that.*'

He glowered at her scornfully. 'Not what, Ruby? Shock? Apprehension?'

'Try horror and contempt,' she bit back, refusing to back down. Hurt still fired her up. 'Try suggesting I don't continue with the pregnancy.'

So much for that voice in her head trying to reason it through earlier.

'I never suggested any such thing.' Ivan's eyes blazed like an icy fire that somehow chilled her and burned her all at once. Yet there was no mistaking the hint of relief that rolled in behind his denial. All the same, Ruby wasn't about to let it go that easily.

'You said that me having this baby was unacceptable.'

'I said that having a baby *with me* was unacceptable,' he refuted instantly. 'But here you are, pregnant, and now we must deal with it.'

And what did it say that her heart didn't know whether to plummet or soar? She fought to keep her voice somewhat even.

'Then what are you doing here, Ivan?'

'I'm here to discuss what happens next.'

'Like me moving to London?' she demanded, forcing herself to stay calm despite every nerve ending jolting and sparking inside her. 'That isn't happening. So, what is there left to say? You made your position abundantly clear.'

'On the contrary, I believe you already decided

how I should feel,' he countered, his voice so controlled now that it was almost more dangerous than the emotion he'd shown before. 'You decided how I should react. And when I didn't match the picture you'd built in your head, you simply left.'

She met his gaze, refusing to allow herself to be cowed.

'As you said, you were clear that a baby was unequivocally unacceptable to you.'

'You didn't even give enough time to process,' Ivan growled. 'When did you realize you were pregnant? Did you find out today and rush straight to London to tell me? Or have you been thinking about it for a week? A month?'

Ruby faltered, hating that he might have a point. She scowled at him but when it became clear that she wasn't going to get away without offering some kind of response, she lifted a heavy shoulder.

'About that, I suppose,' she agreed, deliberately not clarifying how long.

She might have known Ivan wouldn't allow that.

'Which one, Ruby? A week or a month?'

'Something between the two,' she admitted reluctantly.

'Yet you gave me an hour,' he pointed out harshly. 'Less.'

The indignation juddered to a halt inside her, and then something that felt a lot like a sliver of guilt slid alongside it.

Maybe he had a point but she was still too wound

up, too hurt, too angry, to acknowledge it fully. Even so, she jutted out her chin defiantly as if that could stop the quiver inside.

'Your primal reaction was to have nothing to do with either of us, so I left. Would you have preferred me to stay and beg you to want us? To cry when you didn't? That isn't me.'

'I did not say I wanted you to beg or cry.' Ivan clenched his jaw, the veins in his neck pulsing with emotion. 'I said I deserved more than an hour to process such a weighty revelation.'

'And what would it have changed?' She threw her hands up. 'You weren't going to suddenly decide this whole situation was one you wanted.'

'Maybe not.' He reined himself in but his voice was still laced with frustration. The tension seemed to radiate off him in waves. 'But I would have handled it better.'

'You still wouldn't have suddenly, miraculously wanted a baby,' she accused.

Ivan cast her a pointed look.

'Do you expect me to believe this is the situation you would have chosen for yourself? An unplanned pregnancy was what you wanted?'

'This baby is wanted,' she reproached him instantly. 'Perhaps it wasn't planned or expected. But it is already loved and cherished. At least by me—and given how close you know I was with my own mother; you should know that is more than enough.'

And what did it say that Ivan instantly straightened, his expression almost softening for a moment? *Almost*.

'I'm sorry. I remember how close you and your mother were when you were younger.' His voice was oddly gravelly. 'I recall how you missed each other every time she was in hospital and you had to stay with us at Vivian's. And then, that last time when…she never came out.'

A hard lump lodged itself in Ruby's throat, and it took her several swallows to push past it.

'Thank you.'

The silence slid around them again, though Ruby was too lost in bittersweet memories to notice it.

She only knew that losing her beloved mother was why her baby *would* know how loved it was. Already.

Subconsciously, she gently cradled her bump, taking a moment to compose herself before lifting her head to Ivan. And then she was taken completely aback by the expression that had etched itself, without warning, into his uncompromising features.

It might have been unreadable to her, but there was no mistaking the fact that his gaze seemed fixed on the small swell that had previously been covered by her loose-fitting top. Slowly, unsure if she was doing the right thing or not, she let go so that the fabric flowed loosely over her stomach again, concealing it. After a moment, Ivan's gaze lifted back to meet hers—his eyes almost black as though he was veiling his very thoughts from her.

'Have you had your first scan yet?' he demanded at length, in a voice she barely recognized.

Ruby nodded, clutching her bag tighter as she wondered if she should retrieve the scan picture for him to see. She couldn't have explained why she decided against it. Her decision was reinforced by what he said next.

'I want to see for myself,' he announced abruptly. 'Now. There must be a private clinic nearby.'

'In the city.' Ruby pretended her heart wasn't hammering out of her very chest. 'I know the sonographer—she was a former colleague.'

And someone she had trusted with the secret. She hadn't wanted to risk the hospital grapevine before she'd had a chance to tell either her foster mother or her best friend. Though now that Ivan knew, she was finally free to tell them both.

'Good.' Ivan nodded his head, seeming more himself now that he had a goal. 'Then we'll go now. If I have to use every contact I have to get an appointment, then I will.'

And Ruby didn't doubt it though she pretended that it didn't make a difference to her either way.

CHAPTER FOUR

'THE LITTLE TYKE is definitely hiding their face from us.' The sonographer laughed softly with Ruby as she attempted to find another angle. 'Let's try this way.'

Ivan didn't join in. He couldn't. Not when every part of him was so consumed with the tiny life on the screen in front of them. A baby.

His baby.

It shouldn't be possible yet there it was. Despite every vow he'd ever made his entire life, he was going to be a father.

He couldn't mess this up.

Not like his own sorry excuse for a father had done.

But the thought filled him with absolute terror. Dread. Yet something else besides. Ivan shook his head as if that might make it clearer, but it didn't help. He couldn't quite grasp it.

It had been one thing to hear Ruby telling him that she was pregnant, another to spend hours in his car trying to process it as he'd raced up to Little Meadwood, and yet another to see the small swell when Ruby had cradled her bump back at the cottage. But it wasn't until the ultrasound earlier that

Ivan thought he'd really started to understand what was happening.

The 4D scan they were doing now was an added bonus, but it was the small scan picture in his pocket that he kept clutching, tighter and tighter, as if every time he did so he could gain a little more clarity. *That* had been the moment when things had started to shift in his head—though he had yet to make sense of them.

This tiny nectarine-sized thing—almost nine centimetres long—had impacted him more than anything else had ever done in his life before. Growing perfectly, just as any parent might hope for. And that heartbeat…

Ivan had thought he might explode at that rapid, deafening sound that had cracked his formerly impenetrable chest. A tattoo that had seemed to slide and creep inside that black hole within him, and fuse with his own heartbeat. Making him feel… strange.

*Changed…*somehow.

And he feared he would never again be the person he had been only hours before.

No...not exactly feared, *more...something.*

He couldn't even begin to explain, and he was still struggling to understand how such a tiny thing could have upended his perfectly ordered, sanitized world when the appointment was suddenly over and Ruby was thanking the sonographer for fitting them in at the end of her packed evening of scans.

Somehow—he wasn't entirely sure how—Ivan managed to sound half-normal as he added his gratitude to the conversation. And then the woman was gone and his car was plunged into silence as he focused on driving Ruby—and their precious bundle—back to Little Meadwood.

His baby. *Their* baby. It had a placenta now. And it was swallowing amniotic fluid. It was weeing. It was a living being.

What was he even to begin to do with that knowledge?

Ruby spoke of family, but what would he know of that? For the second time today, Ivan found his brain sliding back to Maksim. To wonder what had happened all those years ago. Almost instantly, however, he slammed the brakes back on.

What was to be gained from going down such a road?

It was only when he had parked outside the darkened cottage and Ruby coughed awkwardly that he realized they still hadn't spoken a word.

'Are you coming in?' she managed, her voice throatier than usual. 'Or do you want to head straight back to London?'

He turned his head to look at her and it felt like a century or more before he could actually focus.

'This is our baby, and I will not be an absent father.'

He wasn't sure who he took by surprise more

with the admission. But it was Ruby who broke the stunned silence.

'I'm glad you want to be a part of this baby's life. I truly am.' She licked her lips nervously. 'But I cannot leave Little Meadwood. It's my home, and it want it to be my baby's home, too.'

'I see that.' The words were out of Ivan's mouth before he even realized he was going to say them. 'We will have to find the right solution.'

'Yes, the right solution,' Ruby echoed, and despite her attempt at cheeriness he could hear the tightness in her voice. The uncertainty.

Wordlessly, he unbuckled his seat belt and exited the car, moving automatically around to open Ruby's door and help her out. Still, in silence, he followed as she let them into the cottage and then bustled quietly around turning lights on and closing curtains.

Then she turned to face him—back in the compact living room where their conversation had left off only a couple of hours earlier—and he finally began to speak again.

'I have a good practice in London, and financially I can ensure our child wants for nothing. But I cannot give this child love the way that you can. I know nothing of that kind of thing.'

A thousand words—explanations—slammed against his brain. He ignored them. He had never voiced them to anyone before; it wasn't as though he was going to start now.

The only thing he ought to be focused on right now was that he was going to become a father—the one thing he'd always sworn to himself he would never be. Yet instead of a curse, it suddenly felt like a release.

It made no sense. He was lost, completely out of his depth, after a lifetime of ensuring that his life was *just so,* with nothing in it that could ever disturb the equilibrium. A baby was the very antithesis of that. But instead of loathing every moment of this unplanned revelation, it felt like an opportunity to change something he hadn't even known he would want to change. Like an unexpected freedom from a cage that he hadn't even known he'd been trapped inside.

An invisible cage of his own making—and he'd been oblivious to it.

And it was that particular realization that made Ivan feel unseated and toppled above all else.

Ruby watched the series of complex, unreadable emotions scud over Ivan's perfectly hewn features, wholly captivated despite herself.

The day had ended up so far from anything she had possibly imagined when she'd finally summoned the courage to slip behind the wheel of her car in the early hours of that morning and make that drive down to London—and to Ivan's clinic.

That note in his voice when he'd finally seen the scan and truly seemed to appreciate that she was carrying his baby had made her chest thud so loudly in her chest that she'd been shocked the entire clinic hadn't heard it.

But what did all that mean for her—for their baby—now?

'I'm glad you wanted the scan today,' she began. 'And I'm glad you want to be a part of its life. But I still cannot move to London with you.'

Though it was an internal fight for her to ignore the part of her that was almost tempted.

'I will not be an absent father, Ruby,' he bit out. 'I will not settle for a part-time role in my child's life.'

'Then move to Little Meadwood,' she blurted out before fully knowing what she was about to say.

He stared at her incredulously.

'Why on earth would I want to do that? What can this place possibly offer?'

'Love,' Ruby answered simply. 'Family. Home.'

'And a draughty old cottage that you've shared with Nell since you were both students? I would have thought that you should welcome finally moving away.'

'Then you would have thought wrong.' Ruby folded her arms over her chest, furious and indignant all at once. 'I already told you that this is my home. I love it here, next door to Vivian, where we grew up. Or have you forgotten?'

'I have not forgotten anything,' Ivan snapped, but Ruby refused to hear the distaste in his tone. 'Vivian was the best thing about this place.'

'Then what could be better for my child than also growing up here?'

'Growing up anywhere but Little Meadwood,' he responded coldly. 'Let me clarify that Vivian was the *only* good thing about this place. This is no place to raise a baby.'

And Ruby's heart jolted right there, in her chest.

'This is *exactly* the place to raise a baby,' she managed through a mouth that suddenly felt full of marbles, or something equally unpalatable. 'For the last time, it's my home.'

'But it is not mine.' He began to move then, slowly but inexorably. 'My home is London, where my clinic is. My career. And where people do not stick their noses into other people's business.'

'Is that what this has all been about, Ivan?' she asked when she could stand the silence no longer. Tentatively. Guardedly. 'Your fear that people might see the scars you still carry from your childhood?'

'You have no idea,' Ivan answered flatly.

'Why wouldn't I? We were both Vivian's foster kids.'

'For very different reasons,' he shot back. 'You don't really know my story.'

'Because you've never talked about it,' she pointed out. 'Not when we were kids. And not in the couple of times we've met since.'

Certainly not that night they'd raced to their former foster mother's hospital bedside, only to end up seeking solace in each other's arms.

'Then it should come as no surprise that I have no intention of discussing the past now.'

But despite the harshly uttered words and the tautness in every line of his body, Ruby was sure she didn't just imagine that flicker of vulnerability in his usually black eyes.

It pulled her up sharply, like a douse of a fire extinguisher on the flames of her perceived injury. She'd known how damaged he had been as a teenager; she should have realized some wounds ran deeper than they first appeared.

As a kid, she had never really seen it. He'd been Ivan. Angry, rebellious, dissentient—the bad boy of so many teenage girls' dreams. But now, as an adult, she was suddenly beginning to see that mutiny for what it had truly been.

A kid who had never really known love. Vivian had only had a couple of years to undo the damage caused by a lifetime with a cruel father, or caught up in a terrifying system. Why had she let him fool her into thinking that he was beyond that now?

Little wonder that Ivan's instinctive reaction was that the baby would be better off without someone like him as a father. Her heart ached for him despite her earlier anger.

'I'm sorry,' she forced herself to say. 'I know you have your demons.'

Ivan's gaze was like a silent storm, the pained expression clouding his features reaching inside of her and squeezing even harder than before. And then he clenched his jaw and shot her a look so jagged that it practically pinned her to the floor.

'There is nothing to be gained from dwelling on a long-gone past,' he growled. 'I am here to talk about the future. *My* child's future, to be more accurate. I will provide for this child in a way that neither of us ever had.'

'A few hours ago, you didn't even want to be a father.' She held her hands up. 'I got that. But I want to be a mother so—'

'What I want is neither here nor there,' he cut her off. 'I will be a father—I have seen that scan of my child. I will not turn my back on them.'

And his voice resonated with a sense of duty that both reassured and unnerved Ruby. She had always admired his sense of responsibility, even if it often bordered on self-imposed burdens. But right now, she had no wish to hear him talk about her baby as though it was nothing more than a duty.

For a moment, back there, she'd actually thought something had changed. That a part of him might just be starting to open up to wanting this. She silently begged him to give her a sign—any sign—that this would ever be more than just him doing the so-called right thing.

But he didn't.

It was enough to make her chest pull painfully, squeezing her heart tighter than any fist. As if it wanted to make her explode from the inside out.

How she longed to turn on her heel, run up to her room, and just cry the frustrations of the day away.

Even though she never cried. And she still owed it to him to hear him out.

'That isn't necessary.' She shook her head back, thrusting away all the emotions that swirled around, threatening to choke her words. 'We didn't plan this baby, and having it is my choice, and my choice alone.'

'That isn't how it works, Ruby,' he ground out.

'Well, it can be how *this* works.'

'No.' His jaw tightened, his tone offering no room for argument. 'It cannot.'

The tension cracked through the air between them, a palpable force that seemed to push at the very walls of the small cottage.

'Ivan…'

'This child will have the family that neither of us ever had,' he continued as if she hadn't spoken. As if he *needed* to get his words out somehow.

A surge of conflicting emotions cascaded through Ruby. His intentions might be coming from a place of responsibility, and even a twisted sense of honour, but she couldn't shake the feeling that this decision was being forced upon him. The weight of expectations—her expectations as much as anybody else's—was pressing down on Ivan.

Her fault.

'Ivan, listen to me.' Ruby ruthlessly steeled herself against showing any sign of vulnerability. 'I appreciate your desire to do right by this child—I do. But forcing yourself into a role you don't want will only lead to resentment and pain for all of us.'

'I rather think it's too late for what you or I want, don't you?' His eyes drilled into her, and she was sure she could see the invisible war he was waging against himself. 'This baby deserves a father who will protect it. And I must be that father.'

'But you don't *want* to be that father,' Ruby repeated, her voice cracking for a moment.

Still waiting.

Still hoping.

Ivan's jaw tightened, yet she was sure she didn't imagine that flicker of something unexpected in his eyes. *Regret?* Surely not—and then it was gone.

'But I will be a father,' he stated flatly. 'And this child will have a family. You will move in with me and we will be a family together. Before the month is out.'

Shock jolted through her. The words hung heavily between them, laden with implications Ruby wasn't sure she could immediately process.

'A month? That's what you're giving me?'

'It's thirty days more than you gave me,' he countered unsympathetically.

Her mind raced.

'I never expected you to uproot your life, though, did I?' she retorted.

He arched one dark eyebrow.

'Did you not? The thought hadn't even crossed

your mind when you drove to my clinic this morning to drop your bombshell on me?'

'Of course not,' Ruby cried automatically.

But to her horror, her voice didn't hold the level of indignation she expected. In fact, if she wasn't mistaken, there was a hint of hesitation in it.

Ivan's gaze skewered her to the spot.

'I thought as much,' he noted evenly. Too evenly. 'One month, Ruby. To speak to who you need to speak to. To work your notice. But be warned, if you haven't come to London by then, I *will* come and get you. And you may not like the very public way that I might do it.'

Then he was past her, out the door, and gone. Before the surge of defiance had quite risen within her.

Which might well have been a good thing, given the sliver of doubt that lurked beneath everything, that tiny voice needling her, and asking what she truly *had* wanted, when she'd started out that morning.

What had she wanted to achieve when she'd decided it was finally time single-minded, never-a-foot-wrong Ivan Volkov knew that he was about to become a father?

Perhaps she ought to have been more careful about what she'd wished for.

CHAPTER FIVE

'THIS IS GAVIN, thirty-one. At approximately 22:15 this evening he was travelling on his motorbike at around fifty miles per hour when a car pulled out in front of him. He swerved to avoid it and ended up going into a telegraph pole. Accident was witnessed by a car travelling the other direction who stopped to call the ambulance and police.'

'Right,' the consultant running the show nodded to the ambulance crew to continue with the handover whilst Ruby was already getting to work doing their own preliminary observations and hooking their patient up to the hospital's monitors and drips.

She usually loved her job as a senior charge nurse in the Accident and Emergency Department of City Hospital, but the past couple of weeks—ever since Ivan had left her cottage with his ultimatum—had been more fraught than usual.

She still hadn't made her decision on what she was going to tell him—*if* he even showed up again—just as she hadn't managed to bring herself to tell either Vivian or Nell her news. What if she took Ivan at his word, and acted accordingly, only for him to decide that he preferred to stay away? To pretend that night had never happened?

On the other hand, if he had been serious about

giving her only one month, then her time was running out. Fast. Already half of it was gone, and she was still paralysed with indecision.

It certainly didn't help that there was a traitorous part of her that actually *wanted* to do exactly as he'd suggested. Give up Little Meadwood and play house with the man who was father to her unborn baby.

As if playing at the fantasy of togetherness could ever really match the reality of a happy, loving family unit. She was a fool to think the two were the same thing. At least in the meantime she had her patients to focus on.

Lowering her head and throwing herself into her tasks, Ruby hurried around the department, almost thankful for the distraction. By the time the ambulance crew had completed the list of top-to-toe injuries, and treatment provided, her head was back in the game and the consultant was turning to her for her initial survey.

'Airway's clear,' Ruby confirmed. 'Trachea central, and ultrasound confirms some free fluid in the abdomen.'

She stepped back to offer a clear view of the monitor as one of her colleagues continued with blood pressure and heart rate, whilst two more colleagues confirmed the visible top-to-toe injuries—the most obvious of which was the wide, deep gash on his face which had been lucky to miss his eye by a scant millimetre. Clearly it was going to need significant surgery, but it was the least of the man's injuries at this moment.

'Okay, so we really need to get him up to CT as soon as possible,' the consultant confirmed with a nod. 'See what's going on inside his abdomen.'

Working quickly and efficiently, the team set out about their individual tasks to get their patient ready to move. They were a slick, well-oiled machine that had multiple moving parts all working as one. And, within good time, they were in the CT department with their patient in the scanner.

'Several facial injuries,' the consultant noted. 'Some spinal fractures, too.'

'I'll alert the plastics and neurosurgical teams,' Ruby confirmed.

'Please. Otherwise the volume of fluid in the abdomen isn't as much as I had feared. Possibly he has stopped bleeding, but we'll need to keep an eye on it. I'm concerned he took most of the impact of the collision to his face.'

'Understood.' Ruby nodded. 'I'll accompany the patient back to A&E and get that dealt with.'

For the next hour or so, Ruby worked between this patient and another patient who had been admitted with a punctured lung and broken leg following a fall from a second-floor balcony. Then Gavin's parents arrived, panicking when their son couldn't answer their questions.

'It isn't unusual,' Ruby reassured with a gentle smile. 'Gavin has been in quite a bit of pain, which we're managing. But it does mean he won't have taken in all the information at this point.'

'Okay.' The father nodded jerkily, one hand enveloping his son's hand, the other tightly gripping his wife's hand. 'So can you tell us anything?'

'Of course.' Placing her tablet down so that the parents felt comforted that they had her full attention, Ruby offered another reassuring smile. 'So the results of Gavin's CT were sent to our colleagues, and the neurosurgeon wants to take a conservative approach with regards to his spinal fractures.'

'What does that mean?' the father asked immediately.

'It means that there is nothing immediate that they want to do. Once the swelling goes down it will be easier to determine if your son's injuries will heal on their own, or if an intervention from us will be necessary. Does that make sense?'

'So it isn't serious?' the mother asked hopefully.

Ruby lifted her hand.

'It's more that we can't be sure at this stage. We don't want to go jumping in there if intervention isn't needed, but at the same time we need to keep monitoring Gavin in case surgery becomes necessary.'

'Okay,' the father confirmed as his wife offered a jerky nod.

'Gavin?' Ruby smiled encouragingly at her patient.

'Okay,' Gavin managed, the pained expression

in his eyes almost gone now that the morphine was controlling much of the pain.

If it hadn't been for the degloving, he might have even looked peaceful. Inspecting the ugly wound, Ruby smiled encouragingly at him and carefully replaced the bandage.

'For now, we are more concerned with the impact to your face, Gavin. Our plastic surgeons have already had a look at the scans so we're just waiting for them to send someone down.'

'They are going to deal with it here?' his mother asked.

Ruby shook her head.

'They'll take Gavin upstairs to run their own checks,' she assured him. 'Then, when they are happy he's ready, they'll take him into theatre.'

'Oh. Right.'

'You're doing well.' She smiled at him.

But before she could say more, one of her colleagues popped her head around the cubicle to confirm the plastic surgeon had arrived.

'Great,' Ruby affirmed, moving back from the bedside to give them room.

Her colleague lifted one shoulder uncertainly. 'Actually, they wanted a word first.'

'Oh?' Surprised, she nonetheless turned to offer her patient yet another reassuring smile. 'Be back in a moment.'

Then, her mind racing—had she done something wrong?—she ducked out of the curtain.

And straight into Ivan.

An unexpected jolt ran through her entire body, her hand reaching out instinctively to steady herself against his chest, which did the opposite of helping matters. Solid, familiar—the heat from his body seeped through his scrubs and into her skin. Into her very veins, it seemed.

Startled, she snatched her hand back again.

'Ivan? What are you even doing here?'

The moment of silence which enveloped her felt like a lifetime until, finally, he spoke.

'I understand that you have a patient for me.'

Her breath caught in her throat as she realized too many people were around—too many interested ears—for him to answer the question she was really asking.

But it didn't make her heart hammer any slower. Dimly—shamefully dimly—she began to put two and two together.

'Wait, *you're* the plastic surgeon I'm waiting for?'

How could that even be?

He inclined his head but didn't answer. And interested ears or not, she couldn't help herself from blurting more out.

'But…your clinic is London.' She wished she could have made it sound less like an accusation.

'I might have been a little…heavy-handed the last time we spoke.' He inclined his head, his voice as low as hers was hushed as he ground out the apology that she doubted he wanted to make. 'So I decided to take a temporary post here to give us a chance to discuss our options properly.'

Ruby wasn't certain she'd heard clearly.

'You can't really mean you're working at City now.' She was struggling to wrap her head around it. 'What about your clinic?'

'My partners have taken on most of my clients in the short term, and the board here has agreed that I can head back to London when necessary to see my remaining few patients.'

She shouldn't be surprised. They'd no doubt bent over backwards to accommodate anything Ivan had wanted, just for the chance to have him at City. Even on a temporary basis.

Even so, if felt surreal. Was this really about trying to make compromises? Or was he just flexing his career muscles and taking control?

'How temporary?' she heard herself asking, as if that was one of the real questions jostling around her brain in that moment.

'That's down to me,' he confirmed with a nonchalance that only served to get her back up all the more. At least, that's what she told herself was rolling through her at that moment.

'And?' she snapped, not sure why she felt quite so edgy.

Perhaps it was because of this skittering thing that was now darting around inside her chest. Something she couldn't quite place, let alone name.

'I haven't decided yet.' Ivan flashed a smile.

'They were only too keen to accept my offer of working here.'

'Of course they were.'

They would have been fools not to. Ivan Volkov was a talented surgeon with a rapidly growing reputation in his field. It would have been quite a coup for City, even for a month or so.

Or longer?

'Why are you going to all this effort, Ivan?' she demanded after a moment.

Ivan shook his head. 'That's a conversation for later. Right now, I believe you have a patient for me to see.'

Surprise and annoyance surged through her. She never, *never* forgot a patient, but this damned man had quite the way of getting under her skin. *Effortlessly*, on his part. It was more than a little galling.

Not that she was about to let him know it.

'Yes, of course.' She pasted a cheerful smile of her own to her lips as she turned back to lead him into the cubicle. 'So, this is Gavin. Gavin was involved in a motorbike accident resulting in a facial impact and some spinal fracturing. The neurosurgical team are also monitoring the situation, but it seems his face took the brunt of the accident.'

'Hi, Gavin, I'm Ivan, a plastic surgeon.' Ivan approached the bed with his usual calm, confident demeanour, which Ruby could see instantly set the other man at ease. 'I hear you've been having an altercation with a telegraph pole. Do you mind if I have a look at your facial injuries?'

'Of course not, Doc,' Gavin replied, his voice slightly muffled due to the bandage.

'Great.'

As Ivan began his assessment, Ruby found herself stopping and watching. He moved skilfully, checking the area around the injury as much as the injury itself, all the while talking to his patient calmly.

Would he be so quietly unperturbed with their baby? Bringing it to her at 2:00 a.m. for night feeds? Changing its nappy at three in the morning? Inexplicably, she imagined so.

And then she berated herself for letting her mind wander to that. It felt oddly intimate. Inappropriate.

Shoving the thoughts away, Ruby galvanized her legs back into motion and stepped forward.

Never mind that she felt like she was spiralling downward, caught up in a potent combination of anticipation and apprehension. Dragging her eyes away, she gritted her teeth and forced herself to concentrate on her remaining tasks. Their patient deserved her complete focus, and that was what she would give him.

And Ivan Volkov be damned.

Ruby's heart pounded against her chest as she rounded the corner to her little cottage in Meadwood, her nurse's uniform slightly crumpled after her long shift.

As if that was what had unsettled her the most.

Practically on cue, the sight that greeted her was unexpected and perturbing: Ivan Volkov.

Again.

This time he was leaning against his sleek sports car, looking completely out of place amid the quaint homes with their blooming gardens.

'Twice in one day,' she managed cheerfully. 'Am I supposed to be flattered?'

'You asked me why I was going to such effort.'

'And you told me that was a conversation for later,' she replied, before darting a look around at the surrounding cottages. 'But you know the neighbours are probably already twitching their curtains, watching us together.'

'I do,' Ivan drawled. 'However, I had assumed you would prefer this conversation to be away from the usual hospital grapevine.'

'Well…yes,' Ruby agreed grudgingly. 'Even so…'

'As for the neighbours,' he continued, anticipating her objection, 'am I to assume no one saw me visit your cottage the other week? Or perhaps they simply assumed I was here for Vivian as I was four months ago, and you're just finding excuses to try to keep me away?'

Ruby bit her lip. He was right. Gallingly. No one had actually seen him the previous occasion, which had to be something of a miracle for a tight-knit community like Little Meadwood.

Though she suspected his mention of four months earlier—the time when they had been intimate—was deliberate, to knock her off guard. Well, she refused to allow him to.

'Must you have an answer for everything?' she asked. Tartly.

'Would you prefer me to flounder and flail like a dying fish in the Meadbrook?'

Despite herself, Ruby let out a snort of laughter. Not only because the idea of Ivan floundering in anything seemed quite preposterous, but also because it snagged up a long-forgotten memory of one of Little Meadwood's most skilled fishermen taking Vivian's raggle-taggle group of foster kids on a much-needed day out to the river.

And even though Ruby was fairly sure all of them had railed against going, each and every last one of them had ended up enjoying it. Her, Nell, Ivan, and some other kid whose name she couldn't quite remember now. The calm and quiet of their surroundings, learning to cast a line, and to reel it in, and then that sense of accomplishment when they had cooked their own catches and eaten them with the bread Vivian had taught them to bake the previous day.

'I'd forgotten about those weekends,' she admitted with a soft smile. 'I think it was the first time

I'd eaten something of my own that hadn't come out of a microwave.'

'It was the first time I realized what it must be like to have a father who cared,' Ivan admitted gruffly.

For several moments they just stood there, watching each other. And remembering.

'Evening, Ruby.' The bright voice of Vivian's neighbour on the other side dragged them back to the present. 'Oh, Ivan…back to see Vivian again? She must be thrilled.'

'Thrilled,' Ruby echoed instantly, plastering a wide smile as she swung around.

'I think she might be asleep, though, love.' The neighbour frowned. 'She was in the garden all afternoon, trying to weed the back flower bed. I think she might have overdone it a bit.'

Ruby groaned through the wave of affection that flowed through her.

'Of course she did.' She shook her head. 'She can't take it easy, can she?'

'Never could,' the neighbour laughed, moving towards her own door. 'You might want to leave it a little longer before you go and disturb her.'

Beside her, she could feel Ivan tense and she knew him well enough to know that he was disliking every second of talking about his foster mother with a woman he barely remembered.

And wasn't that the difference between the two of them? To her, the suggestion was just long-term neighbours looking out for each other. People who cared about each other.

Ruby smiled. This was exactly why she wanted to stay in Little Meadwood. She couldn't imagine the same thing happening in London. In any case, it never had when she had been living there with her own mother. No one had cared when they hadn't seen Annabel or Ruby for days. It was only when her mother had needed to be transferred to a specialist centre for different treatment—a place about an hour from Little Meadwood—that Ruby had realized what it was like to have a community that looked out for a person.

It frustrated her that Ivan didn't see things the same way.

'Will do.' She nodded, flashing the older woman another smile. 'Then I'll tell her off for overdoing it.'

The neighbour laughed. 'For all the good it will do. Anyway, evening love.'

Then she was gone, leaving Ruby no choice but to invite Ivan back into her own cottage. The last place she wanted him to be.

And never mind that voice in her head taunting her otherwise.

So Ruby stepped into her home with the man who had haunted her dreams for longer than she could remember. And who would now, thanks to the unborn baby that they shared, forever haunt her future.

'Are you really going to give up your practice for City Hosptial?' Ruby began the moment the door was closed behind them.

Ivan didn't reply; he simply strode up the corridor to the tiny kitchen and began to put the kettle on, leaving Ruby with no choice but to follow.

'Are you going to answer?' she demanded after a while.

'Tea?'

'Coffee,' she corrected haughtily. 'As usual. Or are you suggesting I must have tea now that I'm pregnant?'

'I'm suggesting that you've run out of coffee,' Ivan replied dryly as he lifted up the empty coffee jar for her to inspect.

'Right,' she grumbled, hating that she felt wrong-footed.

'So, tea then?'

It had never been so difficult to utter a single syllable.

'Thanks.'

She waited as he set the mugs out and dropped a teabag neatly into each one.

'I appreciate that our conversations the other week went badly—'

'You could say that,' Ruby interrupted, apparently unable to stop herself.

'But this is going to be a lot easier if we could move past that,' Ivan continued smoothly.

If it hadn't been for the tic in his jaw, she might have actually believed his casual air.

Still, sniping wasn't going to help the situation. Drawing in a steadying breath, Ruby resolved not to let her nerves get the better of her.

It was hard enough trying to rein in her inconvenient attraction to the man who happened to be the father of her unborn child. Not that she had any intention of letting Ivan know that she was still pining after him like the schoolgirl she'd once been.

'Apologies,' she managed. 'Go ahead.'

Despite eying her suspiciously, he duly continued. 'I've managed to agree to a short-term lease on a house in a village between City Hospital and Little Meadwood.'

And Ruby told herself that her heart didn't just stutter and race.

'How? They're like gold dust.'

Rarer, actually.

'Call it a well-placed agent, and good timing,' was all Ivan offered. 'It makes your commute to work a little shorter, whilst still being within a twenty-minute drive of here. Of Vivian.'

'Wait,' she said and shook her hair out down her back if only to cover for the thrill that darted inconveniently down her spine. 'You expect me to live there with you?'

Ivan's mouth pulled into a tight, straight line.

'Do I need to remind you that you are carrying my baby?'

'Is that so?' Her eyes widened in feigned surprise. Because it was either that or explode with the potent mix of emotions swirling inside her. 'I'm so glad you reminded me. I'd quite forgotten.'

'The amateur dramatics are beneath you,' Ivan replied dryly.

It was all she could do not to flush with embarrassment. She knew he was right, and she couldn't keep avoiding the conversation, but it was so difficult to begin when nothing she thought would stay in place instead of sliding around in her brain.

'Fine,' she conceded at length. 'But you don't need to remind me that I'm pregnant. Or that you are the father. I just don't understand, given your initial reaction, why you insist on this charade.'

'There is no charade, Ruby.' Ivan frowned, setting down the mugs to look straight at her. 'I apologized for my initial reaction but I see nothing to be gained in continuing to do so. For now, I am trying to move forward.'

'You're trying to do the *right* thing by moving us in together. But this is the twenty-first century, not the nineteenth.'

'Why do you insist on fighting me?' Ivan clenched his jaw, and shame rushed through Ruby.

It wasn't Ivan's fault that she seemed incapable of acting rationally around the man—turning back into a foolish, mooning teenager every time he was in the mere vicinity. It was hardly as though he was just going to suddenly kiss her again out of nowhere—not that any bit of her brain imagined that he might, of course—so perhaps if she started acting like the usually responsible adult that she was, then she might finally start to feel like it again.

'You're right.' She lifted her hands in placation. 'I'm sorry.'

He cast her a vaguely suspicious look but, to his credit, apparently decided to take her apology at face value.

'Good, then you will move in tonight.'

'I said I was sorry for fighting you on everything. Not that I would stop fighting you on things that are wrong.' She wrinkled her nose. 'I just don't think that moving in together is a good idea.'

'Despite the fact that you are carrying my baby?' Ivan gritted out. 'We are going around in circles.'

'Because you keep insisting on *doing the right thing*,' Ruby exclaimed, trying to pretend she didn't feel hurt or disappointed by his entirely-too-principled approach. 'But neither you nor I had perfect childhoods. We both know that fathers who don't want to be fathers are better to stay away.'

'For the last time, I will not be an absent father.' He narrowed his eyes at her and she wished—oh how she wished—that she didn't feel so piqued yet so compelled to answer.

'Yes, but moving in with someone should be about wanting to be with *them*. Not about doing the *right thing* for a baby who won't care where its parents live, so long as it is loved. Unconditionally.'

And she hated the heat that flooded her cheeks when Ivan turned his incredulous stare on her.

'I am trying to do the right thing, whilst you are talking about attraction? Lust?'

Heat suffused her cheeks at his tone, but at least he seemed shocked, as though he hadn't considered it before. As though her inability to get over her inconvenient attraction to him fortunately hadn't crossed his mind. Even now.

'Don't flatter yourself,' Ruby retorted, hoping to goodness that her face wasn't as scarlet as it felt. 'It isn't as though I'm dreaming of romantic fairy tales. I just...'

Ivan's eyebrows shot up, his gaze pinning her to the spot right through her weak facade. And that look in them suddenly caused her to turn molten. Right when she least wanted to do so.

'You think I don't feel the same attraction? The same pull?'

If she'd suddenly leaped out of her own skin, Ruby wouldn't have been surprised.

'There's no need to mock me,' she managed. Rather too breathlessly.

But it was only when he blinked that it occurred to her that Ivan hadn't even realized he'd made such an admission.

But did that make it better or worse?

'I should never have said that,' he bit out, abruptly taking a step back as if that could somehow erase the moment.

It didn't. It only intensified it. And now the cottage felt as though it was pulsing with unspoken words.

Ignored desires.

'Let's try to be logical,' Ruby managed desperately. 'We can co-parent without sharing a roof.'

'You're peeved,' he replied simply, as though he was actually…teasing her?

Flustered, she instead resorted to glowering at him in defiance.

'I'm not peeved. I am merely stating facts.'

And if her tone was laced with frustration and something else that she didn't even dare to name, then at least she was the only one who knew it.

Right?

Except that Ivan was studying her with an expression that might have been agonizingly inscrutable, but was also making the finest hairs on her body dance with a kind of excitement. She could feel something dangerously close to desire prickling at her fingertips. In her toes.

'I have no desire whatsoever to live with you, Ivan.' She uttered the words before she could stop herself.

Then despaired of herself at the way her body kicked at the wolfish gleam in his eyes. The one that she had thrillingly put there.

'Would you care to put that to the test?' he rasped.

And she knew that voice. It was the one that

had started things off between them almost four months ago.

She should tell him no. She should stop this.

'Would you?' she countered instead. Far too huskily.

When had he rounded the countertop to stand in front of her? So close to her? She could practically feel the heat from his body.

'What are you doing?' she managed, lifting her hands to push him away.

But she was appalled to see herself rest them instead on his chest. Almost tenderly.

'I believe you know exactly what I'm doing,' he muttered, lowering his head towards hers before stopping. 'But all you have to do is say no.'

'This is a terrible idea,' she argued, but her voice lacked any kind of conviction.

Worse, her fingers appeared to be trying to curl themselves around the lapels of his jacket.

'Dreadful,' he agreed, lowering his head further until his face was within an inch of hers. His hot breath tickled her skin deliciously, as though he couldn't help himself any more than she could. 'But the word is *no.*'

And she opened her mouth to say it; she really did. But as his lips hovered so temptingly close to hers—keeping them so close, yet just out of reach—she found herself reaching up onto tiptoe to close the gap herself.

The kiss exploded straight through her. Intense, electric, and white-hot. A kiss that seemed to crackle with the intensity of a hundred thousand unspoken desires. As though the weekend that they had shared had started something hotter and brighter than Ruby had even imagined, and it had been smouldering away ever since—just waiting for this moment to reignite it. And now it felt wild, and out of control, and Ruby never, *never* wanted it to stop.

It hummed in her body and roared in her ears. It seemed to fill up every possible inch of her, yet still leave her thirsty for more. She'd been reimagining this for the past four months yet somehow her memories didn't seem to have done it justice. Not remotely. Not even that most heady sensation of Ivan's lips moving over hers, his wicked tongue invading her mouth in a way that sent shock waves through her core. To right *there*—between her legs.

And when he slid his hands to her waist and pulled her closer, tighter, her softness seemed to melt perfectly against his hardness, like they had their night together. Like they were meant to be.

Except they weren't meant to be, were they? That had been the most intense, erotic night she'd ever known in her life—but it had also been highly out of character. Of all the times for the rule-abiding Ruby to go crazy, surely getting pregnant with Ivan's baby had to be the most insane.

Somehow—she would never know how—she

managed to pull herself back from the precipice and level a direct stare at Ivan.

'I don't know what we've just proved,' she made herself say, all the while telling herself that this wasn't as big a deal as it might seem.

At least Ivan blinked for a moment, looking stunned before he answered.

'We proved nothing,' he rasped. 'Aside from the fact that keeping things practical between us would be a better option.'

And then he moved back around the desk counter and put as much space between them as he could. If only she knew what he was really thinking.

All the same, Ruby feigned a cheerful smile.

'Practical, yes,' Ruby agreed, fighting with all she had to keep from lifting her fingers to her still-tingling lips.

Because she couldn't let Ivan know just how deeply he affected her. *Still.*

No, she couldn't let him know that at all.

CHAPTER SIX

'IS PLASTICS HERE YET?'

Ruby's stomach growled as she hurried through the busy A&E department and to the central station. Probably not the best idea to skip meals when she was pregnant, but the department had been slammed all shift.

'Not yet,' her colleague answered and shook her head. 'But they said they were on their way.'

'One can only hope,' Ruby muttered, half to herself.

Her patient needed attention as soon as possible but it appeared that the entire hospital was swarming with cases tonight. It had been a particularly nonstop, challenging shift in her department alone, and she was so tired that she was uncharacteristically looking forward to getting through the next hour and to the end of her shift.

Yet in some ways Ruby had welcomed the unrelenting nature of the day. At least it had kept her mind from spinning over her previous encounter with Ivan, almost a week ago now.

And, of course, that kiss.

If she closed her eyes, she knew she would still feel his warm breath on her lips, sending such sinful ripples cascading through her body. Making her feel alive in that way of his which always seemed to go beyond anything she had ever felt before. With anyone.

Which only made it all the more imperative that she create more distance between the two of them.

As if it was that easy, she snorted to herself. He had this infernal ability to make her lose her head every time he was around. She seemed to go from competent nurse, friend, foster daughter, to silly schoolgirl in a matter of seconds whenever Ivan made an appearance.

At least she wasn't the charge nurse for the day, so hopefully, by keeping her head down, she could avoid bumping into the man until she had regained a little of her self-control. And dignity.

The last time she'd seen him he'd been in a neighbouring cubicle with a patient requiring immediate surgery, so with any luck she would be out of here before he returned for another patient.

'How's the young girl in bed six?' She peered over her colleague's shoulder at another of her patients. 'I could nip in and see her whilst I wait for Plastics.'

'Urology finally came down about five minutes ago and took her.'

'Oh, that's good.' Ruby nodded. 'What about bed three?'

'Yeah, you could look in there if you have a moment. Ah, too late, here's Plastics now.'

And Ruby didn't need to turn to know that it was

Ivan coming through the door. She could sense it; every nerve ending in her body seemed to be firing up in response to his mere presence.

How pitiful was that?

Yet somehow—she couldn't have said how—she managed to paste a bright, professional smile on her lips as she made herself turn around.

'I thought you were in surgery already?'

'I swapped with a colleague.'

'Why?' She hadn't meant to ask, but the question had just popped out.

'They hadn't worked on that kind of injury for a while so particularly wanted the case.'

It was a reasonable explanation yet Ruby couldn't help wondering if she'd imagined that fraction of hesitation before he'd answered. Still there wasn't a lot she could say.

'Right.' She cranked up her smile. 'So then are you here for my patient?'

'A serious dog bite?'

If he was as thrown as her, then he didn't show it. If anything, Ivan looked as though she could have been any one of her colleagues.

Which should please her far more than it actually seemed to be doing.

'Yes,' she said and nodded jerkily. 'This way. Patient is Dennis…' She stopped abruptly as she realized he wasn't walking with her. 'Ivan?'

'When did you last eat?'

Turning quickly, she hurried back to him.

'A while ago,' she admitted, hesitancy morphing to surprise when he lifted a sandwich, a bottle of energy drink, and a banana from out of a bag she hadn't noticed before. 'You got them for me?'

'It's unwise to skip meals when you're pregnant.' He frowned. 'It can cause increased risk of gestational diabetes, low birth weight, fetal growth restriction…'

'Decreased cognitive and physical function in the fetus, I know.' She nodded, pulling a face. 'I've tried to get away multiple times but the place is hectic today.'

'You're pregnant,' he countered flatly. 'They need to ensure your medical well-being.'

'But they don't know I'm pregnant yet. I still haven't had a chance to tell Vivian or Nell and I didn't want them to find out from anyone else.' She stopped guiltily.

It might be more accurate to say that with all the uncertainty with Ivan, she hadn't wanted to say anything until it was all decided. But she didn't want to sound as though she was blaming him.

'You have to tell them,' he insisted, though not unkindly. 'In fact, given the circumstances, we should tell them together.'

She wanted to tell him no, that she would do it herself. But actually, it would be nice to have him there—he was the father, after all. And at least they all knew each other.

Would that make it better, or worse?

'Okay,' she agreed and nodded slowly. 'That might be a good idea.'

Ivan dipped his head in concession.

'I was planning on visiting Vivian tonight, so we can do it then.'

'Great.' She pasted a smile on her face, trying to look enthusiastic.

What if they weren't excited for her, given the circumstances? They were her family, the people she loved the most. She couldn't bear for them to ask her if she was going to keep it. Her hand dropped instinctively to cradle her small bump.

Well, she'd have to deal with it if it happened. Feigning confidence, she lifted her head to Ivan.

'Now, let me take you to the patient.'

'Not until you've eaten something.' He was unmoved. 'At least the banana. And you must eat the rest the moment you've handed the patient over.'

'Fine.' Ruby picked up the banana hungrily and began peeling it as she spoke, actually grateful to be able to set her own personal concerns to the back of her mind for the moment. 'So, Dennis is a forty-seven-year-old father, playing football in the park after school with his son when he was attacked by a dog. Lacerations to the glabella of the nose, the left cheek, and down to the carotid.'

'Facial nerve?'

'He can still smile, so we believe it has avoided laceration.'

'Okay. You finish eating that whilst I go and introduce myself.'

Before she could reply, Ivan dipped his head once just as he rounded the curtain, and she heard him chatting on the other side of the fabric.

'Evening, Dennis. I'm Ivan, one of the plastic surgeons here. How are you feeling?'

Ruby bit a grateful mouthful of food, her belly grumbling at the extra wait.

'Better now that you're here, Doc,' the father tried to joke.

'That's always good to hear.' She could actually hear Ivan's cheerful smile. 'And you're smiling, which I like to see. Mind if I just inspect the wounds a little closer?'

Another mouthful of the much-needed fruit, and she could imagine Ivan slipping on a fresh set of gloves and selecting his equipment from the tray that she had set up. By the time she had finished the banana and taken a drink before ducking into the cubicle, Ivan had already begun carefully lifting the flaps of damaged skin across the patient's face, working methodically from right to left. Despite everything, Ruby found herself mesmerized by his characteristic skill and focus.

'Can I just ask you to raise your left eyebrow for me?' Ivan asked after a minute.

Ruby watched as the man moved his face, but the eyebrow didn't really lift.

'And again,' Ivan encouraged, keeping his expression neutral when again nothing changed. 'And the right one again? Okay, that's good.'

Wordlessly Ruby prepared to update the patient's notes.

'Zygomatic nerve appears fine. However, frontalis branch on the left-hand side appears to have some contusion,' Ivan stated evenly. 'So, we'll look at that once in surgery.'

'Will you take him now?'

'Yes, the sooner I start, the better the healing should be.'

Calling in a couple of colleagues and working together, it wasn't long before their patient was ready to be wheeled out to the operating rooms, with her colleagues moving first, leaving her and Ivan momentarily in the patient bay together.

And Ruby couldn't explain why her heart was pounding so loudly in her chest like some distant drumbeat. She'd been half expecting it when Ivan stopped and turned back to her, leaving her helpless to deny the flutter in her stomach.

'And after we've got the conversation out of the way with the others tonight,' he gritted out unexpectedly, 'we should start again. You and I.'

Opening her mouth to answer, Ruby was horrified to realize she'd somehow been robbed of the ability to speak. She bobbed her head instead.

'A chance to *reset*, if you will,' Ivan continued.

'That would be...welcome.'

'Good. Then when are you off duty next?'

Her mind raced with conflicting thoughts but she finally managed to find her voice. 'Once I finish this shift, I have a couple of days off.'

'Ah, I have to return to see a private patient the day after tomorrow.' It was nice that he actually looked disappointed, before appearing to have a thought. 'How do you fancy a trip to London?'

London? Her stomach flipped over and she automatically opened her mouth to say no, but something stopped her. 'With you?'

'Like I said, I have to see a patient the day after tomorrow. But I think getting out of this place might help to press the reset button.'

The noise in Ruby's head cranked up, but she had to admit that it made sense.

'So…we would stay overnight?'

Together?

'My apartment in London is two-bedroomed,' he answered simply. As though reading her thoughts.

Lord, she hoped that wasn't true.

Particularly when heat pooled between her legs at the mere discussion of bedrooms.

She pretended not to notice. This was Ivan, the father of her unborn baby, not some… Well, whatever. Her brain floundered for a moment, searching for the neatest way out of the situation. But none came.

In fact, all she could hear was the little voice in her head whispering that maybe getting away from anyone she knew wouldn't be a bad idea. To maybe help clear her head. Especially if she was going to finally tell Vivian and Nell tonight.

She loved them both dearly, but they would each have their opinions on what she should do for the best—with the baby, and with Ivan—and Ruby wanted the space to make her own decisions, uninfluenced by anyone else.

And also, how could she expect Ivan to consider returning to Little Meadwood if she refused to even consider a short overnight trip back to London?

Hastily, Ruby summoned as cheery a smile as she could manage.

'Okay, we said this was a reset, so why not?'

His mouth quirked in a half smile of delight.

'Good. I'll finalize the timings tonight, when I've had the chance to make a few calls.' He tapped his screen with his pen. 'Now, before we see this patient, you need to eat your sandwich.'

She glanced at the forgotten item.

'Of course.'

But Ivan was right; she had to take care of herself. For the baby even more than for herself.

'In fact, you eat it now before some other patient comes in, and I'll go and prep for Dennis.'

Ruby watched him walk away before beginning to unwrap the baguette sandwich he had so thoughtfully brought her.

The more she got to know Ivan—the adult Ivan—the more he surprised her, and she found it a thrill to discover these new layers to his personality that she had never seen before.

But did that mean she was ready to spend a night with him in London, even if his apartment *was* two-bedroomed? She wasn't so sure.

But then again, she was hardly calling him back to tell him she'd changed her mind, was she? So what did *that* tell her about herself?

In that moment, Ruby couldn't say she cared to analyse it.

It had been an interminably long half hour, with Ivan feeling caught between Ruby and Nell, in Vivian's living room, as they waited for their former foster mother to finally feel ready enough to come downstairs.

How many times had the three of them sat in this tiny room over the years? Hundreds of times? A thousand? Including four months ago. Only it had never been so difficult to try to make small talk.

The ease they normally shared was eluding him tonight, and he knew Nell suspected something was wrong. Neither of them could have missed the fact that Ruby had twisted her sleeve into knots, waiting for their former foster mother to finally wake up and head downstairs.

He didn't need her to say anything to know that Ruby was wondering if they should leave their baby revelation for another night. Part of her would no doubt have liked nothing better, whilst it was obvious to him that another part of her could feel the news bubbling inside her, threatening to spill out any moment to the curious Nell.

He actually thought she was on the verge of blurting it all out when the doorbell rang, interrupting the moment and having Nell launching to her feet like the proverbial scalded cat.

It wasn't lost on Ivan that apprehension had seized Ruby the moment her friend rushed out of the room and down the hall to answer it as she turned slowly to face him.

'I'm not sure this is the right time.'

'I don't think it's ever going to be the *right* time,' he countered. 'But don't you think we owe it to them to tell them before they find out by themselves?'

'I guess so,' Ruby agreed grudgingly. 'But this was about telling Vivian and Nell, not whoever that is, crashing the party.'

Then she stood up and smoothed out her trousers in a trait he was beginning to recognize only too well as she cast an anxious look at the door.

Waiting to see who came through it.

But no one did. If anything, it sounded as though Nell was having an oddly hushed conversation on the doorstep.

'Perhaps we should send out a search party,' Ruby grumbled after another few moments.

Ivan merely offered a half smile. He hated waiting, especially with something like Ruby's pregnancy, which felt as though it was burning a hole in his chest. Vivian had been so good to him over the years that he hated the idea of keeping anything from her.

But he had no idea how she was going to react to the news.

'Perhaps tonight isn't the best timing, after all.' He leaned forward to Ruby. But whatever else he might have been about to say was cut short as Nell could be heard heading back down the hall with the impromptu guest audibly in tow.

'I should introduce Ruby,' Nell announced, stepping through the door. 'And Ivan. Both were also former charges of Vivian.'

Ivan stood up out of habit, then stared in shock at the man who stepped through the door.

A face—albeit slightly older—that was instantly recognizable, even though he hadn't seen it in about twenty years.

The silence rippled around the room. And then, before he could swallow it down, a gruff, incredulous laugh escaped him. Just as the other man did precisely the same.

'Ivan?'

'Connor?'

It was the last person he'd expected to see after all these years. But oddly, it was the one person he would have wanted to see, if he'd ever thought about it.

Connor Mason was the first person he'd ever

met in Little Meadwood, besides Vivian. A couple of years older than he had been, and the lifeline he had needed.

As if on autopilot, the two of them stepped towards each other. For a split second, Ivan almost extended his hand in greeting and then, before he realized it, the two of them were embracing each other in a wide bear hug.

It was as if the past two decades had simply fallen away. Just like that. If he'd ever wanted to tell anyone the news about Ruby and the baby, then it would have been Connor.

'How long has it been?' Ivan growled at last, not sure how he even managed to speak.

'Too long.' Connor's voice rumbled with emotion. 'Decades.'

Ivan shook his head, still trying to process as the shocked silence wound its way around the tiny cottage room.

He might have known it would be Nell who broke it. She had always loathed anything she found too tense, no doubt a result of her own experiences of coming into foster care.

'I'd forgotten that you two had known each other.' She offered a slightly shaky laugh. 'But I'd never realized that you'd been so close.'

Without meaning to, Ivan glanced at Connor only to find his old friend staring back at him. And in that moment a whole history seemed to pass between them. But how did he begin to put into words the bond they'd forged? The way they'd had each other's back against the animosity from a handful of born-and-bred Little Meadwooders who had insisted the two of them were nothing more than outsiders?

As stragglers from Vivian's new waifs-and-strays project, how many black eyes, bruised ribs, and fat lips had they endured, sticking up for each other when no one else would? Despite everything, Ivan found himself grinning at an equally amused Connor.

'You could call it that,' Connor finally confirmed to Nell gruffly.

And Ivan wasn't surprised when both she and Ruby chorused their curiosity.

'What does that mean?'

Ivan didn't answer. He would let Connor answer that one, since Connor had always had it worse than Ivan had, possibly because he'd been that little bit… wilder. Probably just because he'd been the first kid the incredible Vivian had taken on full-time.

'It means that if any of the local kids started beating on one of us, then the other would have his back…' Connor offered simply in the end.

'And that was good enough.' Ivan stepped in—his way of assuring his one-time buddy that their old secrets remained just that. *Old secrets.*

Nonetheless, both Ruby and Nell continued to eye them curiously for several more moments until they finally realized nothing more was going to be said.

'Right.' Nell dipped her head at last.

'Okay.' Ruby nodded, as if that was it.

But Ivan couldn't shake the feeling that she was holding on to the unexpected revelation. Or that the conversation would come back around one way or another, once they were alone.

And he wasn't sure how he felt about that.

It was more than a little bit of a relief to hear Vivian making her way downstairs, and Ivan couldn't keep a genuine smile to himself as all four of them leaped up instinctively to help her. It was only the fact that Nell was closest to the door that made the rest of them stand reluctantly back.

He could only imagine what their quiet conversation was that had Vivian chuckling cheerfully through her wheezes as she headed down the hallway, and then into the room.

Her illness was taking more of a toll on her with every passing week, yet Ivan wasn't surprised when their former foster mother defiantly batted away any attempts to get her to sit down, instead taking in every one of them in turn.

And the love that shone from her eyes had Ivan swallowing hard, despite everything.

'Well, if it isn't my favourite foster kids,' she rasped, her delight evident as she stepped forward to hug Ruby, then himself.

'You always say that to all of us,' he rumbled in amusement as he enveloped her in his arms.

And his chest kicked painfully at just how tiny and fragile she felt in his arms.

'Doesn't make it any less true,' Vivian chided with a smile he felt even through his T-shirt. 'Just means I am truly blessed.'

Wordlessly, Ivan released her and guided her to turn slowly to the figure behind the door. He could only imagine how touched she would be to see him again, after all these years. And when she breathed Connor's name, her voice rattling with intense emotion, Ivan felt it in his own heart.

How close had the three of them once been? A makeshift family of two damaged, lost, angry boys and Vivian, the anchor that had kept them all together in the tumultuous sea, helping them to weather the storm.

'Hey, Vivian.' Connor seemed to hesitate only for a moment before enveloping her in his arms. And Ivan wasn't certain which of them was lending support to which.

Either way, it felt like an age before he finally released her again.

'You look good, kid,' Vivian rasped, her voice filled with love that was so familiar that it caught Ivan by surprise.

But then, perhaps it was just the unexpectedness of the situation. Coming here tonight, he simply hadn't been prepared for Connor to appear. It was raking up memories that Ivan had thought long-buried. Memories that he didn't want to have to deal with right now, or perhaps ever.

The homes he'd had before the Vivian-Ivan-Connor years. The places and people he didn't care to think about.

Lost in his own thoughts, Ivan missed the conversation between Connor and their former foster mother, only tuning back in when he realized the other four were all beginning to settle back down in their seats.

What had he missed?

He dropped down quickly into his chair, trying to look…normal. But when he glanced up, Ruby was watching him curiously.

Shrewdly.

'Are you okay?'

Ruby's question was quiet enough, but still he jerked his head around the room to indicate the others.

'Connor and Vivian are intent on catching up.' Ruby shook her head, murmuring quietly. 'And Nell looks a world away. Perhaps tonight isn't the best time after all.'

He hated to agree, but what choice was there?

'Perhaps not,' he managed to grit out, frustration surging through him.

There was a brief beat before she spoke to him again. 'We could try again tomorrow?'

He eyed her sharply. 'Second thoughts about London?'

She had the grace to flush. 'I did wonder if it might be wise.'

'Are you worried about the conversation or staying overnight in my apartment?'

'It isn't that,' she began, before hastily lowering her voice. 'Okay, maybe it's a little of both.'

He could understand that. Curiously, he felt a little strange about the idea of spending the night in his apartment with Ruby. It wasn't that he didn't think he could control himself—he wasn't a neanderthal—so much as he didn't understand why the notion of being so close to her, without actually being with her, should fill him with such…regret.

'I promised separate bedrooms, and I meant it,' he told her with as much enthusiasm as he could fake. 'But let's be fair—what is the worst that could happen anyway? It isn't as though we would be worried about pregnancy.'

And he should be ashamed of himself for the little squeak of shock that slipped from her lips. He hadn't exactly set out to tease her—actually, it wasn't his usual serious style—but he had to confess to a punch of delight when she surreptitiously slapped his arm in silent rebuke, then smothered a giggle.

'So I'll send a car for you tomorrow at nineteen hundred,' he confirmed quietly when they had both stopped trying not to chortle like naughty schoolkids.

She blinked at him in surprise.

'You'll send a car? I thought you'd be driving.'

He could have, but instead he'd planned something better. And he could pretend it was about practicality and saving time—deep down, he suspected it was more about wanting to impress the woman sitting across from him.

Ivan pushed the notion aside and tried to focus on the mundane.

'Nineteen hundred.'

Again she hesitated, and he fancied he could see how she was torn between what the sensible thing to do might be, and what that traitorous part of her longed for. And then her hazel eyes snagged his and for a moment he was lost—right up until she spoke again.

'Nineteen hundred,' she echoed at length. 'I'll be there.'

But strangely enough, he didn't feel any more orientated.

CHAPTER SEVEN

RUBY WASN'T ENTIRELY certain how she managed to keep walking steadily across the tarmac of the private airport where the chauffeur-driven car had deposited her and towards the sleek helicopter that awaited her.

She clutched her small overnight bag even tighter. It had taken all day to pack the thing, second-guessing, then third-guessing every choice she made when usually clothing decisions weren't something that particularly took up much of her time.

Except when it came to staying the night at Ivan's London apartment, apparently.

Little wonder that her heart was hammering so loudly against her ribcage that she feared it might drown out the rhythmic *thwop-thwop* of rotor blades slicing through the air, whilst the setting sun cast a golden hue over the powerful machine, making its fuselage glint in a way that Ruby couldn't decide was more like a promise or an intimidation.

Either way, she had to keep her eye on the goal. To press that reset button whilst also setting up boundaries for her and Ivan. This was their chance to come up with a solution that was both elegant and efficient.

So why, when Ivan leaped down out of the machine—with a casual confidence that held no trace of that odd tension of the previous evening—did her legs almost stop working altogether?

'This is yours?' she managed in disbelief, shouting over the noise.

'Shared between a couple of clinics.' He shook his head. 'Some of our patients who value their privacy the most prefer us to visit them away from London. Helicopter is the fastest way to reach them.'

'And you get to use it at night. For…well…not a date, but…'

'Not as a rule,' he supplied with a smile. 'But as I mentioned, I'm meeting with a private client tomorrow, so this counts as a work flight. Ever been on one before?'

'Never.' She shook her head, her voice a mixture of excitement and trepidation though she doubted he could hear her.

'You'll be fine,' Ivan shouted again, his smile warm as the corners of his eyes crinkled in a way that made him appear less the daunting surgeon and more the boy from Little Meadwood who she remembered fondly.

Then, helping her into the helicopter and sliding in beside her, he adjusted her seat belt before signalling to the pilot that they were ready.

As the other man began to talk into his headset, Ivan adjusted Ruby's own kit, ensuring she could hear him properly. And then they were lifting off. The cityscape shrank below them, a miniature world retreating into the embrace of twilight. Ruby pressed her forehead against the cool window, her breath fogging the glass momentarily as she watched the sprawling lights of the city give way to the countryside.

She didn't know if this was meant to impress her, intimidate her, or something else entirely, but trying to work it out was just sending her head into a spin along with the deafening noise of the blades. In the end, she decided that the easiest thing to do would be to simply give in to the luxurious element of the evening and enjoy it.

When she did, she realized that, strangely, the loud roar of the helicopter seemed to be just what she needed to get out of her own head—if only for the fifty-minute-or-so flight—and Ruby found herself getting lost in the breathtaking scenery skimming past far below her. The twinkling lights of the city gave way to the deep black of the local reservoir, and the beetle-like cars were left behind by the hillside shadow of their aircraft itself.

There was something incredibly powerful about being up here, so high above her normal life. She couldn't put her finger on it, but it made her feel more in control than she had felt for quite some time. So for the better part of an hour Ruby found herself getting lost inside her own head, captivated by the world below her. Rolling hills, farms, the odd village which might look pretty but surely couldn't be as beautiful as her beloved Little Meadwood, which Ivan loathed so much, until at last the bright lights of London came into view.

Then, oddly, her insides did a little dance at the sight. From up here, it looked nothing like the London she remembered. From this distance, it looked like some hidden, sparkling gem far removed from their demanding lives at City Hospital. Almost magical—so very different from the London that she and her mother had experienced. Yet it wasn't this enchanted vista that Ivan loved about the place but rather the capital's anonymity.

Rather like Ivan himself. This was so...*him*, dropping in on the city by helicopter, enjoying selective elements of the place, but as though he wasn't really a part of it. Just as he did with Little Meadwood.

What was it about Ivan that made him so reluctant to actually call a place *home*?

A touch of sadness flitted through Ruby as she pondered such thoughts, unable to shake off the nagging question. It lingered in her mind even as the helicopter continued its descent towards a rooftop landing pad.

And what did it say about her that she was still drawn to Ivan's enigmatic aura even as he kept her at arm's length? How could they possibly raise a baby together when he wouldn't ever let her in?

By the time the helicopter landed, Ruby's mind felt like a dizzying whirlwind. She tried to focus on unbuckling her seat belt but her mind might as well have still been spiralling somewhere above her head, much like the whirl of rotor blades.

Allowing Ivan to help her down on the ground, she let the cool breeze rake over her skin before letting him lead her to the steps where a well-suited security guard waited for them. As they walked down the steps, Ruby couldn't help but steal glances at Ivan, his profile even more mysterious than usual, in the dimly lit evening.

Had she ever really known this man?

She was beginning to suspect not. Unconsciously, Ruby wrapped her arms around herself. The nervous flutter in her stomach hadn't subsided, but it was no longer due to the helicopter ride, and now it made her shiver.

'Are you cold?' Ivan asked instantly.

Then, before she could respond, his jacket was draped over her shoulders.

'Thank you,' she murmured, not wanting to explain what had really caused the shiver. Besides, the fabric was still warm from his body heat, and the gesture had been so instinctive, almost tender.

Or was that her imagination again?

'Shall we?' He extended his arm, and she slid hers through it, allowing him to lead her inside where the atmosphere enveloped her at once, then she gasped.

'Oh…'

She might have even stopped on the spot, had it not been for Ivan's solid, reassuring hold on her.

He leaned down to murmur softly in her ear, 'I remember you once told Vivian that when you and your mother lived in London, you used to pass this place and wonder what it would be like to eat here.'

Ruby stared at him incredulously.

She just about had a dim recollection of the conversation, though it felt about a thousand years ago. Maybe two. How had Ivan possibly remembered it?

A whole cocktail of emotions sloshed inside her, threatening to spill out if she wasn't careful.

Somehow, she made herself take one step. Then another. And each became mercifully easier, until they had finally reached their quiet, private table and Ivan was politely nudging aside the maître d' to pull out her chair for her himself.

'Thank you,' she managed, sitting down and struggling to take it in.

The place. And the company.

Fortunately, the cocoon of soft music and low, intimate conversations in the air around them helped to create a sense of warmth and privacy, aided further by the soft glow of artificial flickering candles which cast a romantic ambiance over the room.

'When you said we should press the reset button,' she ventured as Ivan settled down in the other seat at the table, 'this isn't exactly what I thought you meant. Have you ever been here before?'

'Do you mean, have I ever brought a date here

before?' Ivan asked. 'If so, the answer is no. I just wanted to do something special for you after how badly I've handled things.'

'It wasn't just you.' Ruby pulled an apologetic face.

'You felt protective when you thought I didn't want this baby. That's nothing to regret. And perhaps you were right when you said that I allow my own past to cloud *my* feelings.'

'I never really knew that much about your past,' Ruby began, sitting forward as she tried to find the right words to ask Ivan about his childhood.

She should have known that he would never allow that.

'Like you said—' he picked up the menu, his tone holding a clear note of finality '—it's all in the past. But this is about the future.'

And Ruby fought to quash the sense of disappointment which poured through her at that. Clearly there were things that Ivan would never share with her, and she had to stop hoping that he would.

The waiter arrived to take their order, interrupting the silence that had settled between them as they perused the menu. Ruby settled on the grilled sea bass with capers, confit potatoes, and tomatoes whilst Ivan chose smoked duck breast with a duck leg ragu.

And then the waiter left them alone again, and as Ruby searched for a way to continue the conversation, Ivan gestured discreetly around the elegant restaurant, at the exquisite artwork adorning the walls, and at the plinths.

'So, is this place everything you expected it to be?'

She cast a thoughtful glance around. 'I don't know,' she answered honestly. 'My mother and I used to concoct our own ideas of what it must be like in here, but as time went by, we allowed our imaginations to run wild. I never dreamed I would ever dine here, so I think I forgot long ago what I *actually* thought it would be like in reality.'

'You didn't promise yourself you would return one day, as an adult, and finally find out?'

Ruby lifted her eyes to the chandeliers overhead that cast such spectacular, shimmering patterns over the room—if only to keep back the tears which had unexpectedly pricked her eyes.

'I once promised my mother I would bring her back to London for one Mother's Day, or birthday but…after she died, I swore I would never return again. Ever. I think that was when Little Meadwood really became my home.'

'And you've never left.'

Ruby couldn't have said why she bristled at his tone. Or rather, she didn't care to.

'You make it sound like I'm scared to,' she said and scowled.

'I never said that.'

'But you implied it.'

Ivan eyed her for a moment. Perhaps too shrewdly.

'Or maybe it's something you feel deep down, but are too afraid to admit.'

There was no reason for her temper to flare at Ivan's words, and yet she could feel it puffing up inside her. And she never lost her temper. Another uncharacteristic effect this man seemed to have on her. His words cut through her as effectively as his surgeon's scalpel, and with every bit as much skill-exposing vulnerabilities she had thought long since healed.

He smiled then, though she could tell it was forced by the taut lines at the corners of his eyes.

'But we're at risk of derailing this evening before it has even started. How are you feeling?'

Back to the baby. Ruby tried to ignore the pang of disappointment at the abrupt shift in the conversation. Once again, Ivan was pushing her away whilst appearing like he wasn't—the way he always did.

All the same, she summoned a smile and tried to look unbothered. There would be nothing to gain from ruining the evening before it had even begun. Perhaps there was a way to get him to talk a little more about himself without the conversation going too personal.

'I feel fine.' She nodded, still trying to work out how to steer the conversation. 'No cravings. Sometimes I feel like I'm getting more tired than usual, but usually it's okay. What about you—how are you finding City? I realize it isn't the same as battlefield injuries but it must be different going back to traumas rather than the cosmetic procedures you've been specializing in these past few years.'

'Actually, I've quite enjoyed it.' Ivan looked thoughtful, taking her cue to discuss himself rather than the pregnancy with surprising ease.

As if he knew what she was doing and was obliging her. Even so, she was gratified when he launched into a couple of amusing anecdotes, and by the time the waiter brought their meals, the evening was mercifully back to an easier footing. She found herself fascinated by the subtle nuances in Ivan's expressions, like the way his eyes lightened when he laughed, or the imperceptible softening of his features when he spoke about his work.

Their conversation continued to ebb and flow throughout the meal, a delicate dance of pleasant conversation punctuated by occasional amusing memories of their time together at Little Meadwood, but nothing too deep.

For almost three hours they talked, ate, and enjoyed each other's company. Then, as the last notes of the piano's latest piece faded into the intimate hush of the restaurant, Ivan leaned back in his chair, his gaze drifting beyond the window, where the distant city lights glimmered like stars grounded to earth.

'This place has been a haven to me for the past couple of decades,' he announced, the soft confession surprising Ruby.

Almost as though the hours of uncomplicated

conversation had brought them naturally back around to this.

'London has?' she prompted gently when he didn't continue. 'Why?'

'I don't know.' His fingers played idly with the stem of his glass, the motion betraying a rare moment of self-reflection. 'Perhaps I like the fact that no one really knows me in a place like London. No one looks on me as the kid who everyone abandoned.'

'Not everyone,' she reminded.

He drew in a deep breath. 'No, not everyone. Vivian was always there for me. But…'

'Other people made you feel like you weren't worthy?'

'No.' He frowned, then inclined his head to one side. 'Yes. Probably.'

Ruby reached out and laid her hand lightly on Ivan's. The weight of the words hanging between them was a reminder of the wounds he carried from his past.

'I'm sorry you had to go through that,' she said sincerely.

'Well, I wasn't the only one, was I?' Ivan met her gaze. 'You, Nell, all of Vivian's kids…we all had our battles.'

'No, but some were lonelier than others, I think. At least Nell and I had families who loved us before…they were taken from us. You didn't have that, did you?'

And she didn't miss the flicker of vulnerability that darted across his dark eyes before he shut it down.

'But we survived.' Ivan let the words roll off him, still refusing to let anything penetrate that armour of his. 'That isn't what defines us now.'

'Maybe not, but pretending it didn't happen doesn't mean we have dealt with it.'

She was pushing him, but she couldn't seem to help herself. Surely if they—if she and her baby—were to stand any chance of connecting, really connecting, with Ivan, then he was going to have to confront his past at some point.

Wasn't he?

Ivan fell silent, clearly not wanting to talk any further. His gaze locked on to some point beyond the hushed restaurant, beyond the clinking of cutlery and distant chatter, which seemed to fade into the background as Ruby held her breath hoping that any moment, he might knock down even just one of his walls and finally let her in.

The wiser part of her knew she should let it go. Give him his space. But how could she when it could be the difference between making him a father and making him a good father?

'So how is being back there after all these years?' Ruby began tentatively again.

She wanted to ask if that was why he had ended up with her that weekend he'd visited Vivian. Had she been a distraction for him? It would make sense.

'It's fine, though I never expected to see…' He tailed off, raking his hand through his hair as the casual mask finally slipped.

And though she tried not to, Ruby couldn't help but seize on the chance to exploit it. To maybe understand Ivan just that little bit better.

'Connor?' she supplied, struggling to keep her voice low. 'It must have been odd seeing him turn up like that last night.'

'I guess.'

Clearly Ivan wanted to change the topic but she couldn't let him. She was too desperate to know more. It felt like she kept getting tantalizing glimpses of who Ivan had become, but nothing clear. Certainly not enough to build a fuller picture—and she wanted to so very much.

For the baby's sake, of course, she assured herself quickly.

'Were you close?' she pressed carefully.

Perhaps losing him afterwards was too hard. Had Ivan finally felt like he'd had someone on his side at Little Meadwood, only to lose him when Connor had moved on?

'No.' Ivan shrugged, then relented. 'I guess so.'

'How close?' she pressed. 'Friends? Brothers, even? I know Nell has always been like the sister I never had.'

The expression that scudded across Ivan's face caught her completely off guard. His eyes darkened, like a squall whipping up without warning, and as his jaw tensed Ruby found herself holding her breath waiting for him to speak.

'We *were* like brothers,' he bit out harshly, as if every word was like glass in his mouth. 'But he wasn't the brother I never had.'

'Oh.' She tried to nod with sympathy, but Ivan was still speaking.

'Mainly because I already had a brother.'

CHAPTER EIGHT

IVAN WISHED HE could take the words back even as they left his mouth.

Why had he said that?

He never talked about Maksim. *Never.* It had always cut too deep, and the guilt had been almost crushing. But Ruby was right; Connor's unexpected appearance the night before had caught him off guard. Slicing open a cache of memories that Ivan hadn't been ready to see—especially when he was still reeling from that damned scan.

His fingers clutched the picture that was in his pocket, and had been in his pocket ever since the ultrasound—not that Ruby needed to know it.

He wasn't ignorant to the fact that Ruby's ploy to get him talking about himself—which hadn't fooled him for a second—had ended up working with surprising success.

The evening hadn't gone at all as he'd planned. But then, he'd noticed that every encounter he had with the woman seemed to veer off on a path of its own. Usually everything in his life was carefully arranged, planned out, yet Ruby Channing had an uncanny knack for turning things on their head.

He wanted to say he didn't like it. But even now, when her shock was evident and her hazel eyes were widening as she stared at him before setting her wine glass down, when she gave him her full attention, he found himself helpless to do anything but wait for her to answer.

He tried to take some comfort in the fact that she clearly hadn't known that much about his past, which meant that no one else at Little Meadwood was likely to have known, either.

The way gossip worked in the tiny village, a part of him had always wondered whether, at some point over the years, the truth had come out.

'I didn't know that.'

And he wondered if that changed what she thought about him.

'Does Vivian know?' she asked when he didn't elaborate.

'I have no idea,' he told her honestly. 'I always assumed she did though I never talked about him.'

And when he lifted his head to look at her, the empathy in her expression shook him to his core.

'Then she couldn't have known.' Ruby managed. 'She would never have taken one of you without the other, surely.'

The words hung on Ivan's lips but he couldn't bring himself to say them out loud. Instead, he found himself becoming lost in memories that Ruby wouldn't even begin to fathom. The weight of the world—the entire universe, even—seemed to hang in the air between them. And when he finally began to speak, each syllable was just a little bit too measured. Too loaded with long-suppressed emotion.

'We weren't both in foster care,' he gritted out. 'At least, not in the beginning.'

Yet despite best efforts to keep his tone level, he was certain Ruby could hear that faint ache beneath it, the one that would betray the depth of the wound that ran too close to the surface. The trauma that had festered, untreated over too many years.

But there was nothing he could to about that now. He was the one who had raised the subject of Maksim—he still couldn't have said *why*—so he couldn't realistically shoot down her questions now.

And, right on cue, she reached her hand across the table.

'What happened, Ivan?' she asked softly.

He stared at her long, elegant fingers, wishing he had the strength to lift his own hand and take them. Instead he simply drew in a deep breath, then another.

'I wouldn't even know where to start.'

'Then start with his name,' she suggested with a kindness that almost cracked his chest apart.

'His name was Maksim,' Ivan rasped at last, though it didn't feel like him talking. It felt odd, mechanical, as though his mouth was moving without his consent. And the name lingered in the room like a ghost long forgotten. The spectre that was always crouched there, deep in his chest, finally out in the wild for others to see.

'How old was he?' she encouraged.

'He was three years younger than me.'

And there was nothing to prepare him for the tsunami of pain that crashed over him when he summoned—possibly for the first time in over a decade—the laughing dark eyes of his impish little sibling.

Or worse, the agony and terror that had blackened them when their cruel father had got hold of him.

Ivan clenched his jaw so tightly that he was shocked it didn't shatter right there, at the table. The memories were too sharp, too raw. Even now.

'You were clearly very close, as brothers go,' she offered softly.

A statement rather than a question, though Ivan nodded once, tersely anyway.

'Once upon a time.' He wanted to shut the conversation down, but at the same time he could feel words gathering at the back of his mind, in his throat, as though finally waiting to be released. 'Though he was actually my half-brother. My mother died when I was around two and my father remarried. Maksim was my stepmother's son with my father, and she never let me forget it. Let's just say she was an extremely cruel woman.'

'Oh,' Ruby offered quietly.

Ivan hesitated another moment. 'Home life was the same for both of us, though, but I tried to protect him as well as I could.' He stopped abruptly as guilt sliced through him, sharp and unforgiving, causing him to choke out the final admission. 'Until I betrayed him.'

What wouldn't he have given to be able to say something—anything—other than that? Worse, the expression in Ruby's eyes suggested she didn't even believe him, and Ivan wasn't sure whether that was what tore him up the most.

'But there is nothing else to say,' he declared, shutting the conversation down coldly. 'It is in the past. Done with.'

Except that it wasn't, was it? He'd spent over a decade and a half pretending it was. Thrusting it to the back of his mind.

But then Ruby had told him she was pregnant, and just like that, all those old, unacknowledged feelings of guilt and shame had clawed their way out of the black pit of his soul. As if they had just been waiting for this moment to finally reassert themselves.

All he wanted to do was squash them back down again. He might have known that Ruby wouldn't let it go so easily.

'Tell me more, Ivan,' she pressed. As if she actually cared.

And though his head told him it was a bad idea, Ivan found himself obeying. The words tumbled over each other as he struggled to organize his thoughts into some kind of order.

'I don't know what to tell you… Maksim was

smaller than me, and not just because he was three years younger. He was always thinner, weaker, probably because at least I'd had the love of my own mother for the first two years—not that I remembered her. But Maksim's mother was nothing like that. She met my father a couple of months after my mother died, and Maksim was conceived shortly after, though being pregnant is far from being a mother. She forgot to feed me, or wash me—or couldn't be bothered to—and it was no different for Maksim from the moment he was born.'

Ivan stopped; the jumble of thoughts were still tangled up his head. But Ruby didn't rush him. She just sat quietly, watchfully, waiting for him to continue in his own time. And that somehow made it easier.

'Anyway, Maksim's physical deficiencies only seemed to make our father despise him all the more. I tried to protect him from them—taking the beatings so that he didn't have to. And I learned to steal food from wherever I could. Shops, neighbours, anywhere.'

'My god, Ivan. How old were you?'

Ivan faltered. How old had he been when it had started? He couldn't remember. There had been a time when his father hadn't beaten him—when his mother had been alive, apparently—but he didn't remember it. As far as he could remember, his entire childhood had been centred around avoiding the raging beast that had drunk, and gambled, and snored in his TV chair.

What else had there been to remember about the man?

'I don't know. But the last time it happened, our old man had discovered I'd stolen his beer money. I should have known better, it was a stupid error of judgement, but Maksim was hungry and I was desperate.'

'Your father must have been livid.'

'He was.' The truth was that he'd been so crazed that Ivan had been convinced the old man was going to kill him.

As it was, a tornado was whipping up inside him with every word he uttered, and Ruby was watching him so intently with an expression that encompassed both compassion and concern. But that only made him feel all the more wretched.

'And no one knew? No one helped?'

'They knew,' he managed bitterly. 'We lived in a small village like Little Meadwood. Everyone knew everyone else's business. But no one helped. No one ever stepped in.'

'Oh.' One short syllable, but it held a wealth of understanding.

'I wish you'd told me all this before.'

'What good would it have done?'

'What good?' She peered at him in amazement. 'It helps explain your career choice in London, your reluctance to return to Little Meadwood, your adamance that this child should be brought up in the city.'

'It doesn't because I don't give it the real estate in my head,' he refuted.

Though he wasn't entirely sure he believed that himself.

For the second time that evening, Ruby reached across the table, her hand hovering but not touching, torn between the urge to comfort and the respect for his boundaries. Ivan couldn't decide whether he appreciated it or not.

'Where is Maksim now?' she asked softly, as if she wasn't certain she wanted to know the answer.

This was the question he'd been dreading, but he forced himself to answer all the same.

'I have no idea. I never saw him after that night.'

'You never tried to track him down?'

There was no accusation in her tone, but Ivan felt it anyway. Like a belt across his cheeks—just as he deserved.

'I tried,' he admitted flatly, hating the fact that he was lying by omission. 'But I never found out.'

'You could try again. There are lots of tracing services out there to find long-lost relatives. We deal with this more than you might think at the hospital.'

'I'm aware.' He had to shut the conversation down.

The room had already seemed to shrink with the enormity of his admission. And his guilt. The things he hadn't said slammed loudly into the walls of his brain, roaring the truth.

He concentrated on running his fingers over the rim of his wine glass, tracing the smooth curve before coming to rest. The soft clink of glass against wood cut through the silence that had settled over them like a thick fog.

'What are you afraid of?' Ruby ventured, her gentle voice pushing against his sense of culpability.

He flickered his eyes up to meet hers. 'It isn't about being afraid.'

She clearly didn't believe him.

'You can't feel guilty over something that you must know was beyond your control.' She spoke gently, her hazel eyes reflecting the light and illuminating her face with hope. He thought that might have been what clawed at him the worst.

'I don't,' he lied again.

It was a deflection, but it was the best he could manage. He might have known Ruby wouldn't be so easily evaded.

'If you don't want the tracing services, there are ways, Ivan—agencies, databases, social media…'

'No.'

One word. A command wrapped in layers of pain, and bound so tightly that it seemed to constrict his very breath.

And he hated that Ruby seemed to physically recoil as though he'd actually hurt her. But then she came back at him, her gaze holding his again.

'You were a kid, Ivan. You shouldn't take it all on as your responsibility.'

'You don't know what you're talking about,' he bit out coldly.

'Don't I?' she asked softly.

He hated that she might be right.

'I don't need you to psychoanalyse me, Ruby.' Ivan pushed back from the table, his chair scraping across the floor with an agonizing screech, and it was all he could do to cast an apologetic look around the room as though it was unintentional. 'I only told you so that you would know who I am, but not everything can be fixed, Ruby. Some things are better left in the past.'

Then, walking around the table to help pull her chair out, he gave her no option but to leave the restaurant with him. Instead of bringing them together, every conversation seemed to push them that little bit further apart.

'Ivan…' As she stood up, she reached out, but he sidestepped her touch, retreating behind an invisible wall that felt miles high.

It was the same armour he always donned, shielding himself from the emotional entanglement of their patients' lives. Only now, Ruby would know that he used it just as much to guard against the turmoil roiling within himself.

'Okay, Ivan,' she murmured as she fell into step alongside him, and they weaved their way through the tables, looking all the world like a normal couple having a normal conversation. 'We don't have to talk about this any more tonight.'

'Indeed.' He offered a curt nod that seemed to push them apart all the further. 'We will call it a night and head to my apartment. I'll see my patient as soon as I can and then we'll fly you back to Little Meadwood.'

He couldn't explain what it meant that part of him wanted nothing more than to bridge the gap between them and pull her into an embrace that promised her the kind of life he knew she wanted—deep down. That kind of undamaged family unit he could never offer her.

Setting one leaden step after another, he somehow managed to navigate them out of the restaurant. No, the evening definitely hadn't gone as planned, and he still didn't know what had possessed him to tell her about Maksim. But at least whatever ridiculous compulsion had overtaken him, it hadn't made him spill the whole truth.

If it had, he didn't think he could have borne the disdain in which she would surely have held him. Or that she might have then passed on to their baby in the years to come.

However much he feared he deserved it.

Ruby surged awake with a jolt, her eyes snapping open to the inky darkness of the bedroom. *Ivan's* bedroom, though he'd claimed never to have used it in all the five years that he'd lived in the apartment.

The place was a revelation. The whole evening had been, really. Ivan had opened up to her in a way that she doubted he had ever managed before, and her heart thudded against her ribcage as she tried to work out what to make of it.

She warned herself against reading too much into it, but it was hard not to—especially when her perfidious heart clearly wanted to take it as a sign. And Ruby was getting tired of the fight. Tired of battling her own desires, and tired of telling herself that Ivan Volkov was nothing more to her than the father of her unborn baby.

The truth was that she'd had a crush on him since she'd been a kid, and no matter how much she tried to pretend that she'd grown up since then, it was becoming obvious to her that her fondness had only matured as she had.

But it didn't mean she had to give in to it—even if him kissing her the other night had only served to complicate the situation further.

And she wasn't naive. Evidently there was far more to his story—parts of his past that he had deliberately skirted—but that wasn't the point. The point was that he had opened that door, if only a crack, to finally let her in. Which was more than he'd ever done before.

It made her feel vulnerable and exhilarated all at once. Like she was walking a tightrope between two lives: her old one in Little Meadwood, with Vivian and Nell as her family, and a life that seemed to be unfolding before her, with her baby and with Ivan.

But was that really even a possibility?

Tossing and turning again, Ruby swivelled her head to look at the clock on the bedside table, the digits glowing 2:17 in the morning—each one a silent sentry in the deafening quiet of the night.

She lay there for another moment, still vainly trying to catch the last tendrils of her dream. The recollection of Ivan's shocking revelation, so raw and unexpected, and the words he'd used had left her feeling as if he'd finally permitted her a coveted glimpse at a hidden chamber in his heart. Something she'd begun to fear would never happen.

All she could hear was the pain in every syllable of each of his words, and the curve of his usually broad shoulders betraying just how much the secret must have been weighing on him. And all she could picture was that long moment when he'd just stared at her, jaw set like granite and eyes hard as flint. He'd been so distant and almost impenetrable, yet the lines on his face hinted at something more—a pain he had never shared with…anyone, it seemed.

But now he'd shared it with her, however limited.

Unable to sleep, Ruby swung her legs over the side of the bed, the cool touch of the wooden floorboards grounding her as she padded out of the bedroom and down the wide, polished-wood staircase.

The apartment was quiet and still, save for the softest of hums of the refrigerator as she made her way towards the kitchen. And everywhere around her seemed charged with ion particles—the fallout from Ivan's confession.

She reached for a glass, filling it with cold filtered water from his fridge, when her ears tuned into a sound that didn't quite seem to fit. Unlike the quiet symphony of nocturnal creaks and sighs of Ivan's luxury home, this sound was more rhythmic, sharper, and unmistakably deliberate. The noise was coming from where Ivan should be sleeping. Her curiosity piqued, Ruby put the glass down and silently moved toward the source, her nurse's instincts melding with something more…personal.

Edging down the hall, she listened closer as she tried to work out the sound coming from Ivan's suite of rooms. There was no light under the heavy oak door, no hint of movement save for the sound that grew clearer with each step closer, and the sound didn't suggest anyone in distress, yet Ruby couldn't seem to make herself turn around and leave. Reaching the door, she lifted her hand, paused, and then knocked softly. The noise inside didn't falter, and there was no responding invitation to enter. With a deep breath Ruby's fingers curled around the door handle, turned it slowly, and pushed the door open with an almost silent *swish*, and she was on to the next, slightly ajar door.

Her breath stilled instantly in her chest, her body immobilized, as she gazed at the scene in front of her. Ivan, stripped to the waist, his sinfully lean muscles illuminated by the moonlight which filtered through the window, was moving around a punchball—dancing really—and knocking it so fast that the movements were almost a blur. Each jab was a masterful combination of speed and accuracy, whilst his focus was absolute and the speed of the beat was almost like an incredible music all of its own.

His short, dark hair was damp with exertion, and the intensity in his blue-black eyes so fierce that she wondered who he was imagining that punchball to be—himself perhaps? His guilt had been unmistakable when he'd talked to her tonight, though she still couldn't understand it. Either way, he was so engrossed in his solitary battle that he didn't notice her standing there until she was nearly upon him.

'Can't sleep either?' she ventured tentatively, her voice steady despite the thunderous beat of her heart.

Ivan's knuckles stilled against the leather of the punchball, his gaze snapping towards her. For a fleeting second, surprise flitted across his features before his usual mask slotted neatly back into place. But it was too late; she knew she'd caught him off guard, and in that brief half a second she had seen a flicker of the vulnerability he so rarely showed.

'Ruby,' he bit out in a neutral tone. 'What are you doing up?'

'I could ask you the same thing,' she replied and shrugged.

His chest heaved with his exertion.

'I'm just getting in a little exercise.' His clipped tone did little to conceal his irritation. She suspected that was intentional. 'I don't need an audience.'

Ruby remained unfazed, recognizing the defensiveness for what it was—a shield against the world. She moved closer, her gaze soft and unthreatening.

'Maybe not, but everyone needs a little company at times.'

'This is not one of those times.' A muscle ticked in Ivan's jaw, the only sign of his internal struggle.

'Perhaps I meant me,' she pointed out, 'rather than you.'

CHAPTER NINE

IVAN DIDN'T ANSWER, but eyed her sharply for a moment. Then, rolling his shoulders to release some tension, he turned away from the punchball to face her fully as the air began to palpably thicken.

She turned away, and he told himself that he was glad. Even so, as she made her way around the room step by step, he couldn't seem to bring himself to drag his gaze away and return to his workout.

Right up until the moment she reached his bookcase.

His breath caught in his chest as she slid her eyes over the items on display. Books, of course, but also some travel pieces, some trophies, and a handful of photos. He watched with mounting agitation as she noted the army photos, the medical pictures, and then that one nugget of history that no one else had ever seen.

Slowly, painfully slowly, he moved towards her as if he could distract her from the inevitable.

Her hands reached out to the old, dog-eared photo even before he was halfway across the space.

'This is you,' she breathed in surprise. 'You're a lot younger than when I first met you but I recognize you all the same.'

'Yes,' he managed, his mouth suddenly dry.

'And the smaller boy next to you?' She lifted her head abruptly. 'Is that him? Is that Maksim?'

Ivan opened his mouth to reply but the confirmation caught obstinately in his throat. It took him several rough swallows to get past it.

'Yes, that's Maksim. It was when a travelling fairground had visited the area and our parents were too boozed up to notice that we'd gone. We sneaked in, and sneaked on some of the rides until the guy taking the photos noticed us.'

'And he threw you out?' Ruby guessed, wrinkling her nose as she examined the photo a little more.

He and his brother were on the wooden horses of a merry-go-round, grinning inanely with little Maksim squinting into the sun. They'd had a lot of fun that day—and none of it legitimately.

'Yeah, he threw us out. But not before he gave us a photo each and told us to use it to remind us that if we wanted to be able to do fun things for real, then we were going to have to work harder than most people, because we were starting off further down the ladder.'

'Oh.' Ruby was careful to keep her expression neutral, though he was fairly sure she wasn't impressed.

In truth, it might have been the best bit of advice he'd ever been given—until he'd been fostered with Vivian. But her lack of understanding only seemed to underscore the difference in their home lives. He couldn't have said why that irked him suddenly.

'Seen enough?' He crossed back to his exercise mat and the punchball.

'I'm here if you want to talk about it,' Ruby ventured, closing the gap between them with a few cautious steps.

Her hand reached out tentatively, hovering just shy of his sweat-dampened arm before making contact. The touch sent a jolt through her and, by the looks of Ivan, it had done the same for him. He moved away, making her feel suddenly cold. Rejected.

'I think I did enough of that earlier tonight,' he ground out. 'And talking doesn't change anything.'

'I don't believe that.' She pulled a rueful expression. 'Maybe I'm wrong but I think you feel differently just for finally letting go of some of the things you've kept pent-up for so long. I think that's why you're here now, unable to sleep, because there's more you want to say. You just can't allow yourself to, can you?'

For a long moment, they simply stood there, the rhythm of their breaths in perfect sync in the quiet room. Close enough that Ruby could feel the heat radiating from Ivan's body, a result of his exertion, and something more besides.

'The thing is,' she began hesitantly when it became clear that he wasn't going to speak. 'We talked about demons earlier, but you aren't the only one who is battling them.'

'I told you, I'm not battling any demons,' Ivan refuted.

But she noticed that he didn't move away from her.

'You say that, but I see the shadow in your eyes,' Ruby told him softly. 'I recognize them from when I look at my own reflection in the mirror. The thought of raising this baby without my mother… without even Vivian—'

She stopped abruptly, biting her lip.

Carrying those fears had been bad enough, but actually uttering them aloud…? It made them that much more real, all of a sudden. Made the situation that much more real.

And still, Ivan didn't answer.

'My mother would have been the greatest grandmother that I could have wanted for any child—just as she'd been the greatest mother I could have ever hoped for.' A lump lodged painfully in Ruby's throat. 'Do you realize that by the time this baby is born, I will have spent more time on this earth without my mother alive, than I had ever enjoyed with her?'

And it stung.

More than stung.

Even so, it was only when Ivan suddenly enveloped her in his arms that she realized how desperately she needed to be comforted. She was only too ready to collapse against him. To draw strength from him. And surely they were going to need each other more than ever now that they were expecting this baby together.

Suddenly, she needed to know more than ever before just how much Ivan was acting out of a sense of duty, and how much he genuinely cared for her. Had it just been that one weekend together? She didn't think so, but she needed to know for sure.

No matter the circumstance, this child *would* be surrounded by people. It would have her, it would have the fun and talented auntie that her best friend, Nell, would surely be, and it would have the loving community that was Little Meadwood.

And even if cruel fate meant that her baby would miss out on knowing how it felt to never know what it was like to have Vivian, then Ruby was determined that she would share as many happy memories as possible.

But, most significantly, this child had a chance to have the father that Ruby herself had never known. A father who wanted to be a part of their life—whether he was doing it out of duty or desire, did it really matter so long as he was actually doing it?

Without warning, Ruby felt herself at a precipice. To retreat would be to return to the safety of solitude, but to move forward could mean embracing something that might be just as real, and true. It was time to let go of the foolish, childlike notions of Ivan falling in love with the idea of a baby, or a life as a family—or indeed her.

Because, whether she'd wanted to admit it or not, Ruby was finding it harder and harder to pretend that a part of her wasn't in love with Ivan.

It had been the case when she was a kid, and it still was now. And she could fight against it all she wanted, but it wouldn't make it any less true.

But that didn't mean that Ivan had to know that. She wasn't a mooning kid anymore. She was a grown woman, mature enough to set aside those unrequited feelings and simply accept what Ivan *was* offering her.

A different kind of life for her baby. Two parents who were working together for their child. Something neither of them had ever experienced for themselves.

'Thank you,' she murmured softly, carefully detaching herself from Ivan's comforting embrace and ignoring the voice in her head that railed at doing so. 'I'm okay now. I think being back here in London, and visiting that restaurant, just reminded me of my mother. It caught me off guard for a moment.'

'You never have to apologize for missing her,' Ivan rasped. 'I know you were her world. I can't even imagine what that would have been like.'

'But we can offer that to our own child.' Ruby lifted her head. 'If I move in with you, then we can create a family unit that may not be like another person's but that works for us.'

'One that has two people both wanting to do the best thing by the child,' Ivan agreed hoarsely.

And she tried not to let her heart race away with her when he gazed down at her, a flicker of surprise and something else she couldn't quite decipher in his eyes.

'It will still be more than either of us ever got to experience,' he continued. 'A chance to break the cycle. For me, at least.'

'Yes. Exactly.'

It was meant to be a moment of clarity; Ruby knew that. But as their eyes locked, she felt something shift between them. Ivan's usually guarded expression softened, if only for a moment, and she caught a glimpse of that well-hidden vulnerability that made her heart ache.

Almost as though he didn't realize what he was doing, he slid his hands to her shoulders, moving her back slightly so he could look straight into her eyes. Before she knew it, Ruby found her own hand lifting to rest against his chest, over his heart as it beat out a rapid tattoo against her palm.

The moments ticked by, unheeded as they allowed the sliver of unexpected intimacy to carry them away. There was a suspended moment where he no longer seemed to be a formidable surgeon, or a haunted former foster kid, or the father of her unborn child.

In this instant he was just a man, raw and open, standing in front of her and stripping her soul bare.

And the world outside—with its demands and demons—fell away, leaving only the connection that they'd allowed themselves to explore once before.

So this time, what more consequences could there be?

Their breaths mingled in the small space between them, the air crackling with a palpable energy, and Ruby couldn't have said whether Ivan ducked his head to her, or she reached up to him, but at last—*at last*—their lips were brushing and they were kissing.

And what a kiss.

He claimed her with fire, and fever, and everything in between. Like the headiest liquor that rolled through her with the most indulgent laziness, and she was already punch-drunk on the taste.

His hand cupped the nape of neck, turning her head this way and that as he tasted her. He toyed with her, and he teased, kissing her so thoroughly, so comprehensively, that Ruby's lips began to tingle under the wickedness of the assault. And still, she was only too happy to revel in every single second of it. Every minute.

And then he shifted.

The small moan escaped her lips before she could catch it—but how could it not when his thigh was suddenly right *there*? Between her legs the hardness of his thigh was pressed so deliciously against the softness of her core. Where that greedy heat bloomed so instantly for him.

Had she moaned his name? She thought maybe she had, but then perhaps it was simply that it flowed through her veins, like an imprint all of its own. Stamping her as his whether he had wanted to or not.

She was ruined for any other man—that much was clear to Ruby. She had been ever since that night several months ago. And likely before that, when she'd first met him as a teenager and fallen head over heels in love.

And as Ivan began to peel her thin nightclothes off—almost reverently as he took the time to explore her changing body, with the curves and swells that bore witness to the life she was now carrying—she could feel that familiar tremble starting low in her belly and slowly moving out of her in waves.

She moved against him, trying to press herself closer. She wanted more—so much more—his hands all over her body. His skin sliding over hers.

'Patience, Ruby,' Ivan muttered as she shifted against him again.

And she took some gratification from the fact that his voice sounded much, much thicker than usual.

Then, without warning, he hauled the last of her clothing smoothly over her head, offered a low growl of approval as he drank in the sight of her, and then bent his head to take one proud, hard nipple directly into his mouth and sucked. Hard.

Ruby almost toppled from the gloriously dizzying sensations right there and then. Instinctively, she threw her head back and arched her back, as if trying to offer him even more of herself.

Ivan seemed only too happy to take it. With one hand splayed over the bump of her abdomen, and the other holding her backside, he appeared to take inordinate pleasure in swirling around the pink bud with his tongue. Sucking her in until he was *just about* grazing the very edges of his teeth in a way that felt wholly sinful, and then releasing her to the cool night air so that her nipple puckered up immediately in response.

Over and over, he teased her. And when she thought he was finally done, he turned his head and repeated the entire delectable process on her other breast. This time when he sucked, it sent such a kick of frenetic desire straight from her nipple to her aching core that she thought she might die from need if she didn't have him sliding inside her.

Now.

'This is wholly unfair,' Ruby gurgled dully when her brain had finally remembered how to make words.

But Ivan only laughed, a dark, intimate sound that sent fresh thrills cascading through her, and carried on. Glutting himself on her as though she was the most desirable creature he had ever known.

Even more than he had last time, she registered dimly. Though she had no idea what to make of the realization. And even less desire to bother trying—not when every lick, and suck, and swirl of his tongue was sending her closer and closer to the edge.

Then, before she had fully registered what he was doing, she found herself lifted up into his arms. Swept through the air like she weighed nothing—bump and all—and then he was carrying her back through his suite.

Ruby had a vague recollection of him shouldering his way through the heavier oak door of his bedroom, and then she was being deposited on a huge, wooden carved bed in a room that felt masculine, yet not too dark. And then she didn't care to notice anything else, because Ivan was pulling off his own clothes and crawling up the bed between her legs—his skin sliding feverishly over hers and his shoulders gently nudging her a little wider apart.

And then, when he was happy where he was, Ivan lowered his head between her legs, and licked her *right there*.

Where she ached for him most.

Ruby almost came apart there and then. Waves of pleasure were assailing her from every angle, but then Ivan slid his hands under her backside and lifted her up to meet him and it all got so much worse. Or better.

Certainly hotter.

She heard herself cry out his name but it all seemed somehow distant. Muffled. As though she was outside her own skin and he was the one who was twisting her inside out. Over and over, he used his wickedly clever tongue to tease her, driving her closer to the precipice than ever.

And then with one last slide of his tongue, one last graze of his teeth, she lost it. She came apart right there against his mouth and his hands, arching her back and crying out his name. All the while he held her. As though she was infinitely precious, and to be cherished—always.

If only that were true.

But there was no time to dwell, because now Ivan was propping himself up between her legs and her hands were already reaching down for more of a touch. If she wasn't pinned so delightfully down beneath him, she might well have taken her tongue and licked all along his hardest ridge. Slipping him into her mouth, tasting him, and enjoying the sight of him losing control exactly as he had just made her do.

And then, the thought was gone the moment the velvet-smooth tip of him nudged at her heat. Automatically, Ruby slipped her hands around his body, over the swell of his biceps and down the ridges of his back muscles. Finally, her name on his lips like some kind of prayer, he slid inside her.

Ruby cried out softly, his sheer maleness sliding into her molten heat—tentatively at first—as though it had been waiting a lifetime. As though they were finally home. Slowly, slowly, he moved in and out, his pace leisurely at first, building up the heat, and sending those waves lapping through her again. Until Ruby slid her legs around his waist and pulled him in harder, meeting each thrust with a faster, harder rhythm. Making Ivan fracture and splinter the way he had done with her.

And when she lifted her hips and dug her fingers into his back, Ruby was finally rewarded as a low, guttural moan was ripped from Ivan's lips and he sank himself fully into her, tossing her straight back over the edge—and following her besides.

Ruby had no memory of falling asleep, but when she woke several hours later to find herself still in Ivan's bed—his body fresh from the shower—she was more than gratified when he hauled her back to him, rolled over, and began the explorations all over again.

If this was what living with Ivan would also be like, then Ruby was beginning to think that the first thing she would do when she got back to her cottage in Little Meadwood would be to pack.

CHAPTER TEN

'OKAY, MIKEY.' Ivan smiled at the fourteen-year-old patient in front of him. 'So Ruby has explained what's happening? You know that although it's quite a clean cut, the wound on your face does go down to the cartilage, so I'm going to have to do it under a general anaesthetic.'

'Right here?' The boy grinned, whipping his phone out now that the examination was over, so that he could take some delightfully gruesome selfies to send to his mates. 'Cool.'

'No, not here.' Ivan shook his head. 'We'll get an operating room prepped for you and get you down there.'

'Sick. Can I video it for my mates?'

Across the room, where she was dealing with the equipment trays, Ruby tried not to look too much at Ivan, but there was no stopping the thudding that started in her chest every time he was near.

After their night together—and Ivan's subsequent patient review—it had been a strange flight back home. They hadn't discussed what had happened, but every brush of their hands had felt deliciously contrived, every glance had felt intensely protracted.

If it hadn't been for the unexpected call just as

they had landed, urgently requesting him to attend an emergency at City Hospital, Ruby still wasn't sure where they would have ended up going next. By the time she'd hurried in to cover a shift herself, her head had been a jumbled mess of excited uncertainty.

It still was—though this wasn't the time to delve into her thoughts. It was almost a relief when young Mikey cut into the moment, lowering his mobile phone from his face.

'Hang on. You say general anaesthetic, Doc, but I'll still be able to get back to rugby training soon, right? We've got a match coming up against Rock Bay Rousters and they're, like, our arch-nemesis. I *gotta* be back in time for it.'

Despite her nervous tension, Ruby smothered another smile. She'd been dealing with the young patient for the previous hour, and she knew what was about to come.

'Not unless your idea of *soon* is several months,' Ivan answered firmly, turning back to focus on his patient. But they both suspected it would go in one of Mikey's ears then promptly out the other. 'This is a traumatic soft tissue injury. Early management has given us our best possible chance of good healing with minimal scarring, but further damage risks additional bleeding, possible airway obstruction...'

'Yeah, but it's the *Rock Bay Rousters*,' the boy exclaimed, slipping the phone away. 'I can't miss that match.'

If young Mikey had made that point to her once, he'd made it ten times already. If nothing else, she had to admire the kid's sense of invincibility as well as his dedication to his team. All she could hope was that he would listen to the advice if it came from a man like Ivan, rather than her.

'Sorry bud.' Ivan sounded sympathetic, yet immovable. 'We can't risk any complications by rushing back, even for the Rousters. Your health and recovery have to come first.'

'Yeah, but I'm a really good healer, you know? I bet you've never seen anyone heal as fast as I do.'

'You'd be surprised.' Ivan plastered another smile to his lips.

And Ruby watched as he patiently explained the risks to Mikey in greater detail. His authoritative yet caring attitude calmed the boy despite the disappointing news. She couldn't help admiring how Ivan handled the situation and clearly the boy appreciated the man-to-man talk—which was fortunate given that the boy's mother was still outside in the waiting room, refusing to come in to speak to her son presurgery as she couldn't bear to see his injuries.

Not that she couldn't do it alone, but it would certainly make it easier to talk to both Vivian and Nell if Ivan was there with her. Hopefully it would make them worry about the situation less.

'I'm going to explain it to your mother now,' Ivan

told Mikey as he finished up with his patient. 'Then I'll get set up for you.'

'Cool.'

Mikey nodded happily, his phone already coming back out of his pocket, and Ivan took the opportunity to briefly indicate to Ruby to join him outside.

She told herself that she wasn't all too eager to oblige. Her heart was thudding in her chest.

'We should talk about the other night,' he noted quietly, after ensuring no one was around to overhear them.

The thuds grew louder but she forced herself to answer.

'Yes. We should.'

'You will move in with me tonight.'

As *talking* went, it was more of an instruction, but Ruby didn't point that out. She was too focused on the detail of what Ivan had just said.

He *did* still want her to move in; the relief was almost dizzying, given a part of her had feared he might have changed his mind after their recent shared night together.

She couldn't have stood it if she'd robbed her unborn baby of its chance of a family—quasi family—simply because she couldn't seem to control herself whenever she was around Ivan.

Not that she had any intention of saying any of that to him.

'Tonight,' she confirmed, wishing her voice hadn't sounded quite so husky. So sultry.

A flicker of emotion chased across Ivan's face before he smoothed it into blankness. Ruby tried not to feel so hurt. Plainly he still wasn't prepared to let her in fully, but she could only hope that he'd be less guarded with their baby, when it finally arrived.

'Have you time for a break after this?' he asked. 'Grab a snack? Make sure you're still eating.'

'Here?'

In the hospital?

Was it really wise to meet Ivan here, where the hospital grapevine would be swinging into action before the two of them even took their first sips? Okay, slight exaggeration, but not far off.

Then again, people were going to have to find out about her pregnancy soon, and if she was going to be moving in with Ivan—*if*—then it wouldn't take them long to fit the puzzle together. Perhaps it was better to get it out in the open and the gossip over with?

'It's just a snack, Ruby,' Ivan's mouth tugged up at the corners as if he could read her mind. 'How about meeting me once I'm out of surgery? Shall we say *Re-cup-eration*?'

'In the downstairs atrium where everyone can see?'

'Well, I don't fancy a vending machine drink. Whatever those things spew out, it isn't coffee.'

'You know that isn't what I meant.' She tried to

pull a face, but her insides felt too fluttery to carry it off.

'You meant because everyone will see us? And because of what happened the other night at Vivian's, you still haven't had the chance to tell her about the baby?' he half teased for a moment before turning serious. 'But time is passing by, Ruby, and at this rate it will be born and I still won't be able to be a proper father.'

Which, she couldn't help noticing, was a complete change from that first day she'd told him the news. Wisely, she kept the observation to herself. She doubted Ivan would welcome the reminder.

'I know,' she conceded seriously. 'I don't want to keep putting it off, but I would prefer them to know about the baby first. Maybe it will even give Vivian a bit of a boost.'

To her relief, Ivan bowed his head in acknowledgement. It was a delicate balance that she was trying to find right now, but if anyone understood why her foster family was so important to her, then it would be Ivan.

On the other hand, it should concern her more that she was increasingly turning to him to provide the support she had initially anticipated Vivian and Nell would show. Despite their shaky start, Ivan had proved to be more of a rock than she could have imagined.

So why couldn't she shake the foreboding feeling that, unless he finally did something to confront his demons—like finally summoning the courage to sign up to a tracing site for his younger half-brother—then they were missing the very foundations for this fragile world they were beginning to build together?

And her fear was that the slightest storm could easily bring it all crashing down.

Mill Cottage turned out to be less of a small, low-ceilinged dwelling and more of a sleek-lined, dizzyingly vaulted open space.

Ruby stood in the hallway; her neck craned right back as she gazed up at the glorious, honey-coloured beams at least eight metres above her head.

'This is what you managed to rent at short notice?' she breathed, struggling to take it all in.

'Like I said before, lucky timing.' Ivan shrugged dismissively. 'And a good contact.'

'One who you now owe a case of wine or something?'

'Probably.' He grinned, leaning against the door jamb and fixing her with a too-direct stare. 'So do you want the full tour, or would you prefer to find your way around in your own time?'

'The tour, definitely.'

Surely she shouldn't be so giggly about the move? It was supposed to be about practicality. Instead, she felt like her insides were fizzing and popping with delight. And it definitely wasn't the baby.'

Thinking about which…

'What about the nursery?' she blurted out excitedly. 'Do you have a room in mind for that?'

Belatedly it occurred to her that Ivan might not be planning that far ahead. With a rush, she considered that maybe he thought they would be out of Mill Cottage and in London by then.

It was a relief when he returned her smile with a wide, apparently genuine one of his own, and lifted his arm to gesture to the upstairs.

'You have three choices of bedroom. Take your pick.'

'Really?'

'And if you want to put your stamp on them, choose some swatches or I can bring in a decorator to help.'

Ruby paused, glancing at him in surprise. 'I can paint?'

'Sure.' He didn't look bothered. 'It's in the contract. As long as we revert everything to its original state when we hand it back, we have free reign. So if we end up staying here a little longer, say after the birth…then at least it can feel like ours.'

That certainly hadn't been what Ruby had expected from him. With each passing day, Ruby was finding it harder and harder to remember that they weren't a proper couple. And that would inevitably be a problem.

She stilled without warning, her mind suddenly opening itself up to the uncertainties that she had been trying to keep at bay. The buzzing was faint at first, but it grew louder the longer she stood still. She felt torn between the joy of planning her baby's nursery and the unspoken doubts that lingered in her mind every time she caught that sad expression of Ivan's that she didn't know he had. Or the way he pulled back from her sometimes without even noticing.

And, her chest heavy, Ruby realized that she couldn't quash it any longer. She couldn't pretend everything was okay. She *had* to say something before she talked herself out of it.

'Ivan…'

But as he turned, swivelling on his heel as he moved to face her, Ruby felt the flutterings she'd been feeling for the past few days—only suddenly, she knew what it was.

She lifted her head to his in shock.

'The baby is kicking,' she managed, grabbing the wall with one hand and her own belly with the other. 'Oh, Ivan. You need to feel it.'

Ivan's expression turned to one of surprise as he immediately stepped closer to her, his hands lifting to hover uncertainly over her abdomen. Ruby couldn't help laughing, her mounting misgivings scattered and lost in the moment. Ivan had likely operated on thousands of patients as a doctor, seen thousands more as patients, but faced with the energetic kicks of his own unborn baby, he looked as startled as any lay father might be.

Carefully, solicitously, she took his hands in

hers and placed them gently on her belly. The baby didn't take long to show off its prowess.

'That can't be… It's incredible,' Ivan breathed, a mixture of emotions scudding across his face.

Suddenly all Ruby could do was nod and laugh and cry all at once—and nothing else seemed as important anymore.

So what if Ivan had his fears—didn't everyone? And did it matter if he didn't want to search for his brother to find out what really happened? Perhaps Maksim had been part of Ivan's old family, but she and their baby were his family now. They could take care of each other—*love each other*—more than anyone else ever could.

And in that moment, Ruby vowed to do just that. She would forget any notion of looking for Ivan's family, and she would concentrate on her own.

Starting now.

So, for the next few hours, Ruby explored her new home with Ivan. She followed him eagerly from room to room, sharing her initial thoughts as each one boasted its own unique charm. One had a large picture window that let in lashings of light, another had beams that snagged the eye and captured the imagination, and yet another had the prettiest built-in shelves that she soon learned housed a hidden door which led to a secret room behind.

When they finally stopped to feel for more baby kicks, Ivan's hand lifting to catch a stray tendril of her hair behind her ear, she gave in to the desire to be intimate with him again. Their bodies were moving together with familiarity but still that same electric thrill. And that connection between them was feeling stronger and more unbreakable by the day.

But Ruby might have known the outside world would come rushing back in sooner or later. And when it did, it would crash over them with an icy reminder of all the questions she'd allowed to go unanswered.

CHAPTER ELEVEN

THE FOLLOWING FEW days bled into the following few weeks for Ivan, with days often spent with Ruby, whether at the hospital or baby shopping; and nights spent with Ruby, whether under him, over him, or in his arms.

It ought to have been hell—this little sliver of unplanned domesticity. But inexplicably, it wasn't.

Not by a long way.

Which might have explained why Ruby was always at the edge of his thoughts. Her sharp wit and killer smile invaded his brain at the most inappropriate of times. And all too often he found himself wondering where she was and what she was up to—wanting to share in her life far more than he felt was appropriate given the circumstances.

Which was ironic, really, Ivan snorted as he vaulted out of his car and into the house that had become far more of a home than he cared to admit.

He found Ruby standing in the room he had earmarked as his office, a patchwork of pastel-hued tester colours dotted on the walls and her head tilted back as she considered each one in turn. And when she didn't see him, Ivan found himself stepping back and indulging in several moments of admiring her without disturbing her.

And no matter that he had no business doing either.

It was only when she began to turn around that he stepped forward as though he had just arrived at the doorway.

'Are we going for a circus theme?'

'Very funny.' She pulled a face. 'But for the record, babies can see brighter colours much better than pastels, especially early on.'

'I'm aware.' He smiled, watching as she dipped her brush into a palette of colours and added another one to the wall with careful, deliberate strokes.

'But this is just for a backdrop to the room. I can introduce high-contrast blacks, whites, reds with accessories like the baby mobile, or bedding.'

'Right.' Ivan leaned in the doorway, watching her despite himself. 'Looks like the beginnings of a masterpiece.'

Ruby glanced over her shoulder in surprise, returning his smile with a bright one of her own that seemed to sneak inside his chest and coil itself around him, her hazel eyes catching the fading light.

'It's got to be perfect,' she replied, her voice light but underscored with the weight of her dreams. She brushed a strand of brown hair from her face, leaving a smudge of lavender on her forehead.

'Any favourites?' she invited him to join in, but he shook his head.

He was terribly afraid that if he pushed off the

door jamb and headed over there, he might do something stupid, like try to clear away that blob of mint green on the tip of her nose which—rather than making her look like a clown—only seemed to make her look all the more adorable.

'Whatever you choose will be fine.' he assured her. 'But I will paint it—don't tire yourself out. I only came in to see if you were ready for the restaurant tonight.'

In a moment of romantic madness, he'd booked a table at the most upscale restaurant in the city, a gesture that he still wasn't entirely sure why he'd made.

But right now, he had the distinct impression that Ruby would far rather stay in, order a local takeaway, and chat at the dining table over a glass of elderflower cordial.

He couldn't say the idea didn't appeal.

'Unless you'd prefer I cancel?'

She pulled an apologetic face, and her tiredness showed for a moment.

'Would you be awfully disappointed?'

'Devastated,' he drawled, loving the way her eyes crinkled up in delight.

Well, not *loving,* he amended hastily as he called the restaurant. But…*appreciating.*

'You might want to get a shower anyway, though,' he teased after he'd finished the brief call. 'You appear to have mistaken your skin for the wall a couple of times.'

How he loved how her cheeks flushed a soft pink

at his mention of the shower, and how endearing the colour looked on her warm skin—like a delicate rose blooming in the early-morning sun.

And he tried not to think about stepping into the large shower enclosure with her as he had the previous night, and making her scream his name even louder. And his body reacted, as it always seemed to do, like an adolescent, at the mere memory.

'Go,' he muttered hoarsely, before his baser instincts got the better of him. 'I'll clean up and get us a takeaway. Any requests?'

Ruby paused for a moment, thinking, a mischievous glint crossing those hazel depths.

'Let's surprise each other. You take care of the dinner, and I'll handle dessert.'

He chuckled at her playful suggestion, feeling a warmth slide through him at the easy banter they shared. It was moments like this that reassured him that family life *could* be different from the one he'd known in his childhood. That he wouldn't perpetuate the cycle of his cruel father.

With Ruby's help.

Watching her move through things with such passion and purpose was like a breath of fresh air in his too-structured life, and he couldn't shake the feeling of contentment that washed through him, especially when he wasn't looking.

He couldn't remember the last time he had felt this level of peace and contentment with another person and it was a peculiar sensation.

He ought to have known that it couldn't last.

* * *

'Ivan, wait. Don't go.'

Ruby halted Ivan as he was heading out of the Resus Department a week later. Tonight he had been home rather than working and still, just as she'd begun to realize that the shift was already half-over and she still hadn't had chance to eat, he had appeared with a home-cooked meal and an instruction to take a break.

Now, moving around to the same side of the desk as her, Ivan lowered his head to her ear and followed the direction that she was watching.

'What is it?'

Ruby pulled a face.

'I don't know. I can't say exactly.' Only there was something in the way a boy in the opposite cubicle—in for a fractured arm following a fall down some steps, as she recalled from her colleague—flinched when his father approached his bedside.

It had been fleeting, no more than half a second, something and nothing that could so easily have been missed given how normal the family had been acting moments earlier, when her colleague had been in the room.

Yet Ruby couldn't shake the feeling of apprehension that had settled in her stomach.

'Do you see anything?' she ventured, wondering if it was just her imagination.

'Yes.' Ivan's low, unhesitating response caught her off guard. 'Whose patient is it?'

Her food once again forgotten, she glanced around for the colleague in question, not surprised to see them caught up with another case. Clearly, they were tied up for a while so did she let it play out, or follow her gut?

Her gut won out.

'I want to head in. You'll observe from here?'

She didn't wait for Ivan to respond before she was hurrying across the floor to the bay, her eyes hastily taking in everything from the way the boy refused to meet his father's eye, to the way he held his good arm across his stomach in an overly protective manner. And another boy—a younger brother, possibly—was perched on a hard plastic chair, swinging his leg whilst apparently not engaging with anyone.

'Are you injured somewhere else, sweetheart?' she asked brightly, ensuring her smile was open and approachable, and not the least bit threatening.

The boys' father was by her side within a matter of a second.

'That's nothing.' He moved his arm as though to form a barrier between Ruby and his son.

Ruby nodded, cranking her smile up further.

'Thank you, but I should like to examine your son for myself.'

'Your colleague didn't need to.' The man didn't move, but his smile set Ruby on edge. 'He ain't complained of no pain other than his arm.'

'No problem,' Ruby said brightly. 'But I *would*

like to just check so that we can ensure you aren't stuck here any longer than necessary.'

The father seemed to take a moment to weigh up her words, though he still refused to step out of the way. His attitude was doing little to ease the tension Ruby felt.

'Is there any reason my colleague shouldn't check your son for other injuries?'

At the sound of Ivan's casual tone, Ruby exhaled the breath she hadn't realized she'd been holding.

The father scowled at Ivan, but Ruby noticed that he moved back an inch. Still, his jaw jutted out pugnaciously.

''e didn't complain of nothing else. 'e just needs his arm sortin' and we'll be outta here.'

'Absolutely.' Ivan moved towards the man in as nonthreatening a way as possible. 'But perhaps, with the obvious fracture of the arm to contend with, your son didn't realize he'd sustained another injury at the same time.'

'At the same time?' the father echoed, the wheels clearly beginning to turn in the man's head, and Ruby couldn't help think he was grasping at plausible explanations for what he knew they would find. 'Yeah, it's possible. Likely, really, now you mention it.'

Ruby watched Ivan handle the tense situation, engaging the man in a calm conversation whilst giving Ruby the opportunity to move around to the other side of the boy's bed. The younger brother was no longer swinging his leg but watching her intently—right up until the moment when she glanced his way and he bowed his head as if he wanted to disappear into the floor.

She turned her attention back to the patient.

'Hey there, I'm Ruby. Mind if I take a quick look at your stomach?'

It tugged at her heart the way the boy refused to meet her eyes; his eyes fixed on a spot on the floor. Keeping her voice gentle and reassuring, she managed to prise the T-shirt from out of the boy's tiny, tight grip and lift it.

Bruises peppered the boy's stomach and chest. Small bruises. And lots of them. Yellow, black, purple, green, all revealing different lengths of time. Not injuries that he could have sustained in the recent apparent fall, but she couldn't afford to jump to conclusions. They could have been sustained from the two brothers having kids' blaster-gun fights, firing foam darts at each other, or…?

But coupled with the boys' demeanour, both terrified and flicking glances at their father and away again, it didn't quite seem to sit right. Her gut was warning her not to let it go. She'd been here before as a nurse. Too many times for comfort.

Ruby tilted her head to Ivan, careful to keep her expression neutral.

'More injuries,' she confirmed in as light a voice as she could. She was still acting as though she believed the injuries had been sustained in the recent fall.

No need to alert the father yet.

Still, the micro-expression that slid over Ivan's features caught her off guard.

She couldn't shake the feeling that this was more familiar to him than he would ever have cared to admit. And though she told herself not to, it was impossible not to watch as he skilfully managed to manoeuvre the resistant father out of the cubicle, still playing along with the idea that the injuries had been sustained that day.

Finally, she hit the bell to summon the colleagues dealing with the case, voicing her misgivings so that they could start their usual procedures.

And this time when she watched Ivan head out of the door, confident that the matter was being handled appropriately, Ruby sucked in a steadying breath and thrust aside her guilt over having filled out the form to enable Ivan to trace the younger brother he claimed not to have seen in almost two decades. After all, what did they say—*it was better to ask for forgiveness than permission*?

Especially when she was pretty much ninety-nine percent convinced that he would *never* give the latter.

Ivan should have taken a bet on Ruby resurrecting the subject of Maksim after the incident with the father and his boys.

He could even have taken a bet that she would raise it that night, as they settled down in Mill Cottage kitchen for their meal. Not that he was enjoying it. Despite the glorious ingredients and skilful cookery, everything tasted bland to him today. He'd be better when he could get to bed and escape into sleep.

Tomorrow would almost certainly be a better day.

'Are you sure you're okay?' Ruby asked for the third time in as many hours. 'I'm here if you want to talk.'

'I don't,' he bit back, before trying to soften it. 'Thanks all the same.'

Still her persistent gaze—so full of concern—threatened to send a crack through the dam of his memories. Abruptly, she pushed her half-finished plate to the side.

'Ivan, I can't just sit back and say nothing,' she burst out. 'I saw your expression with those boys today. I know it cost you to be in that room.

'You're mistaken.' He tried to shut her down but he might have known his Ruby wouldn't be so easily deterred.

His Ruby? Where had that even come from?

'I don't think I am.' Ruby leaned forward urgently. 'Why don't you contact him, Ivan? It's obvious you want to. Your brother clearly meant a lot to you.'

Her words crashed over him like a huge stormy wave slamming into a tiny fishing vessel—like the ones his hated father had once taken them on, forced them on, really. The kind of boats that had always made Maksim so violently sick—and their father laugh and sneer at his youngest son's lack of fortitude.

Wherever his brother was now, Ivan could only hope he was far away from their old life.

'You are mistaken,' he ground out, his eyes finally swivelling to meet Ruby's. 'Tracking down Maksim is the last thing I would ever want to do.'

'Why?'

Exasperated, Ivan dropped his fork onto his plate with a loud clatter. Frustration, fear, and—mostly—guilt all slammed into him at once and made him utter the words he hadn't ever wanted to tell her.

'Because I don't even know that he is alive.'

And in that instant, he knew that even though he wanted to take them back, he never could. Just as he also knew that Ruby wouldn't rest now until she knew the truth.

Standing up as steadily as he could, Ivan gathered their plates together and began heading back to the kitchen—more to take the opportunity to regroup than anything else. But by the time he started to speak again, he had his thoughts more organized in his head.

'I told you what happened the last time I saw Maksim,' he began. 'When I'd stolen the beer money to buy some food and, actually, to pay the meter.'

'You told me your father was angrier than you'd ever seen him before,' Ruby concurred.

'Well, I thought he was going to kill me. So I decided to leave that night and go for help. Get the authorities. Anyone who would listen. I raced out of the house—I banked on the fact that as bad as Maksim's mother was, she would never have let my father actually hurt Maksim—and I ran.'

'And you found help?'

'After a fashion.' Ivan shrugged, trying not to let the injustice of it all permeate his soul, even now. 'I sent them to the house but our parents were ready. They had a story all concocted, about how I was a troublemaker and had been ever since my mother died. They told the authorities that I was a danger to my half-brother, and they even had a couple of neighbours there to lie and back them up.'

'That's horrendous,' Ruby muttered, the fierce expression on her lovely face almost making the unpleasant trip down memory lane seem bearable.

'I was taken into care and they got to keep Maksim. I delivered him right into their hands.'

The guilt and unfairness of it burned inside him even now. Too bright. Too hot. He pushed it aside and tried to focus on Ruby.

'So that was the last time you saw Maksim?' she asked, her brow furrowed as if she actually cared.

'The last time,' he gritted the words out. 'I tried to get back to him that first week. I ran away from the home. But I got caught. The second time I ran was about two weeks after that, but when I got home both Maksim and his mother were gone.'

'Gone?' Ruby cried automatically. 'Gone where?'

And he gave a bitter laugh at the expression on her face.

'I don't know. I asked around. I asked scores of neighbours, but they all said the same thing. That they'd been there one day that first week, but by the time people had woken the next morning, there had been no sign of them.'

Ruby stared at him aghast.

'You don't think…?' She caught herself, shaking her head. 'No, of course you don't.'

'I don't think that my father did anything to them?' Ivan offered a hollow, bitter laugh. 'The thought has crossed my mind.'

'And?' she prompted, clearly unsettled by the idea.

And he liked his Ruby all the more for it.

'I don't know,' he told her honestly. 'There was one neighbour—old lady Craven—who finally told me that she had helped them. She claimed to have kept hold of whatever his mother gathered together to pack, and then helped them out of the village that first night.'

'Well…that's good news, isn't it?'

'It is.' He dipped his head once. 'If she was to be believed—she was never exactly kind to us. But I prefer to think that was what happened.'

'Right.' Ruby nodded slowly. Uncertainly.

And she looked so bereft that Ivan felt responsible.

It was his past, his story, that had cast a shadow over Ruby. This pregnancy should be a happy time for her but his history was tainting it. Just as he'd feared from the start.

Just as it had been for that family in the hospital today.

'And if I agreed to leave it,' Ruby began again, more hesitantly this time, 'do you think it would help? Would you want to move on? Would you feel more inclined to try to see what might have happened with Maksim?'

'It would not,' Ivan clipped out, frustrated that his own shortcomings were making Ruby second-guess her own choices like this.

Maksim was in his past; he didn't want to revisit that. But neither did he want to brush it under the carpet any longer, as if the little boy had never existed.

So where did that leave things?

As much as he was loathe to admit it, perhaps it was time to stop being selfish, and instead to consider whether Ruby and his unborn child were actually benefiting from having him in their lives.

Or whether it would actually be better for anyone if he returned to his distant, isolated life.

'I've missed this.' Nell linked arms with her as they strolled through the park opposite the hospital. 'This morning was mayhem.'

'Tell me about it.' Ruby smiled, squeezing her

friend's arm in return and rubbing her other hand over her eyes, grateful to finally have time with her best friend.

From their time as foster kids together, it had been their weekly ritual to take a walk around Little Meadwood and share any worries or concerns, and offer advice—a habit that had continued until recently.

Until Ivan.

Dimly, it occurred to Ruby to wonder what might be going on in her friend's life right now such that Nell had seemed equally distracted of late—enough that she'd accepted Ruby's absence as a result of crazy overlapping night duties. But her mind was already racing too much with her own worries to really give it more thought.

The unexpected phone call from Maksim had caught her completely by surprise. And now she was supposed to be meeting the man in two days' time—in a city halfway between Little Meadwood and London, where she could be anonymous—so that she could determine for herself whether seeing his brother after all this time might help Ivan or alienate him further.

Right now, she needed a neutral pair of eyes more than ever. But how did she even begin to explain it all to her friend?

'I'm used to Resus being slammed but that was insane.' Ruby tried to keep the small talk going when Nell didn't speak. Tried to sound normal, and in control of her careening emotions—if only to buy herself more time. 'I think there are still roadworks in the city so it has been quicker and easier to get all the emergencies here. And for the record, I've missed this, too. I'm sorry if I've been a bit distant recently.'

'Want to share?' Nell asked, her voice full of empathy and something else that Ruby couldn't quite identify. Suddenly it occurred to Ruby that she might not have been the only one caught up in their own life recently; now she thought about it, recently Nell hadn't been around as much as usual, either—or her friend would certainly have dragged the truth out of her by now.

Ruby opened her mouth, then closed it before rubbing her hand over her eyes again, torn between wanting to blurt out about her and Ivan and the baby. Torn also between the fact that Ivan had a brother, and not wanting to spread a secret that he had clearly kept hidden for a reason.

'It's crazy. And complicated.'

But then, if anyone could offer sage advice, it would be Nell.

'You don't have to feel obligated.'

'I know,' Ruby sighed. 'But… I want to. I just don't know where to start.'

And why did she feel that Nell's nod was that little bit too heartfelt?

'Start wherever feels comfortable.'

Ruby almost laughed. She had no idea where that would even be. Everything was just so…jumbled.

'It's just I've been…wondering about what it would be like to live somewhere else.'

It sounded so much worse, out there in the open. As though she was abandoning the place that had offered her haven after her mother's death. Or was that just her emotions talking?

'Oh.'

It was hardly the response that Ruby had been wanting. Which, in itself should probably tell her more than she'd been prepared to admit.

'Haven't you ever thought about leaving Meadwood?' she asked, trying not to sound too hopeful.

At least if Nell had had the same thoughts, she wouldn't feel so ungrateful.

'Not really.' Nell shrugged.

And Ruby couldn't have said why she didn't believe her. Possibly because her heart was already aching.

All these years and she had never known the truth about Ivan's childhood. She could have been kinder. More empathetic. Maybe she could have even helped—though she wasn't sure how.

But she could help now, if only he would let her.

Deep down, she knew it wasn't her place to push Ivan. Nor was it her place to decide whether his own childhood was affecting his current decisions more than she had realized. The form that she'd filled out on his behalf still weighed heavily on Ruby.

How many times had she tried to find the words to tell him what she had done almost a week ago now, only to lose her courage at the last moment?

The weight of some of Ivan's words still lingered in her mind. That determination not to let their unborn baby grow up the way either of them had—without a proper family. The shocking admission that he hadn't really known anything of love for the first fourteen or so years of his life.

She could still hear that steely note to his voice. The one that told her he'd hated how trapped he'd felt. How helpless. But she also knew what had happened with the boys from the hospital that night—against all protocol, she hadn't been able to stop herself from finding out—and it gave her a small sense of victory to know that they were no longer under their father's control where he could hurt them, but were instead now ensconced with a set of grandparents who loved them and wanted to keep them safe.

If only the same could have been done for Ivan and his brother.

Without warning, her mind slid back to the photo in Ivan's London apartment. He and Maksim with their devilish smiles, having a ball at the fairground and clearly as close as two brothers could be.

And Ruby couldn't ignore the gnawing feeling that until she understood Ivan's past better, she would never fully be able to understand the man who was the father of her unborn child.

Which was why she would be doing the right thing if she met Maksim in London on her day off the next day—however much her conscience needled her that if she did so then she would be acting behind Ivan's back.

Betraying him—which was just about the last thing she would ever want to do.

Shaking her head, Ruby stared across the park, missing half of what her best friend was saying. She needed to tell her about Maksim, and about the past they'd never known about Ivan—if anyone could offer her some much-needed advice, then it would be her former foster sister.

But the words wouldn't come, and Ruby couldn't find a way to express to her friend all the things she really wanted to say. And even though they talked, Ruby wasn't sure she would remember a single word of it afterwards.

But perhaps that was for the best. After all, filling out those forms had been her decision—so it should equally be her decision to meet with the man behind the back of the father of her baby.

And it certainly wasn't fair to now start dragging an oblivious Nell into it all, but Ruby couldn't seem to help herself. She pushed on with the conversation anyway, even though she still had no idea how to articulate her worries.

As if it might somehow reveal answers to the questions she hadn't yet had the courage to ask.

CHAPTER TWELVE

RUBY WALKED IN through the door, throwing her keys on the table with exhaustion.

It had been a revelation of a day, but now she was shattered—drained—and not just because her baby had been kicking wildly at her all afternoon.

Meeting Maksim had been an eye-opener. Half-brother or not, the man was exactly like Ivan, and yet nothing like him. They might look like carbon copies of each other, but there was a softness to Maksim that Ruby had always known existed in Ivan—but that Ivan had long since learned to harden.

A softness that she had been glimpsing more and more often—however fleetingly—in the time she had been living in Mill Cottage.

Maksim had enjoyed a decent life—a far more stable one than Ivan—in the end. But it had been gratifying to hear the other man acknowledge just what his big brother had sacrificed for him.

Now all she had to do was convince Ivan to hear Maksim out, and she was sure—*certain*—that it would be the push Ivan needed to finally break free of his chains and embrace his future.

With her and their baby.

'You're back then?'

She swung around guiltily as Ivan's rich voice sounded behind her. Covered in paint but looking mildly satisfied with himself, he began to advance on her.

'Did you have a successful day?'

For a moment, she floundered. 'Successful?'

'You were looking for some things for the baby, were you not?' His smile was almost indulgent this time.

And as he stepped closer, she found herself leaning in, drawing a kind of strength from the warmth that was radiating from his body. His familiar scent enveloped her, and filled her senses with need and longing.

But she couldn't. She mustn't.

Ivan closed the space between them, his hands sneaking around to her shoulders to pull her back to his comforting, muscular chest.

'You know you are breathtaking when you're flustered?' he teased, his lips grazing her ear.

And she knew she should step away, but she couldn't seem to make her legs move.

'Am I?' she whispered, leaning closer still.

His presence was intoxicating, and Ruby found herself drawn by the magnetic pull of him, despite the voice screaming in her head that this was not the time.

She just wanted this one last moment. This one last, guilty pleasure. After all, what harm could it do?

Their lips met, and the world seemed to fade away, leaving only the sensation of warmth spreading through her veins. And as Ruby clung to him, her fingers tangling in the short strands of his dark hair, his arms wrapped around her and he held her close, as if he were afraid she might slip away.

He was wrong. She had no intention of going anywhere—*ever.* Not when every fibre of her being responded to his touch, affirming that her feelings for Ivan ran to her very core.

They parted, breathless, foreheads resting against each other's. The doubts that had clouded her mind seemed less formidable now, overshadowed by the raw emotion that resonated through her entire body. The way he claimed her as his without even saying a word. What words were needed, especially when his mouth, the way his hand held the nape of her neck, the way his arms had her sprawled against him, said it all?

He kissed her again, and again, and again taking his time, being thorough. Each time more perfectly delirious than the last, and every time that kiss swept over her mouth, demanding more, the fire only seemed to burn brighter in her very being.

'These really do have to go,' he teased, lifting his hands to unhook her top and ease down her jeans.

The clothes fell with a *swish* to her feet, gathering in a little denim puddle that she stepped so neatly out of. And then she heard Ivan's sharp intake of breath, and she felt the tiny grin tug at the corners of her mouth. For there, under the clothes, she was wearing the tiniest scraps of lace briefs, and a lacy bra.

He pulled back from her for all of a second, shedding her of the rest of her clothing with ruthless efficiency.

And then she was standing there naked, in front of him, and not feeling the least self-conscious. If anything, Ruby decided feverishly, she felt wanton, womanly, and wholly desired—especially when he slid his hands down to her gently swelling belly to cradle it with a kind of reverence.

But she was all too hot, too needy, to bear it for long.

'I feel that one of us is wearing entirely too much clothing, and the other too little,' she managed after a few moments, reaching down with trembling fingers to try to remove his paint-splattered shirt.

'That can be remedied,' Ivan growled, shedding the garment in an instant before hauling his shirt over his head.

And her throat went immediately dry at the sight of the man, naked to the waist, standing in front of her with a devilish gleam in his eyes.

Suddenly, before she realized what he was doing, he had hauled her into his arms and was carrying her across the room to the soft couch in the corner only to lay her out like his own personal feast. His gaze slammed into hers with so much desire stamped in their black depths that, for a moment, she thought it might have stolen her breath clean away.

And then he dropped his head and took one proud nipple deep into his mouth—and she knew her breath *had* been stolen.

Need rolled through her like a rumbling thunderstorm, making her judder and shake with every wicked sweep of his tongue. He drew whorls on her skin, hot and wet, then let his teeth graze oh so gently against her—and Ruby thought she might well be burning up from the inside out. And once he had satisfied himself with one nipple, he simply swapped sides and started on the other.

She almost shattered from that alone. But Ivan had other plans. He built her up, higher, and higher, and higher still. Tracing patterns with his tongue whilst letting his hands explore the rest of her. Her waist, her back, and suddenly, her bottom. Too late, she realized what he was doing as he lifted his head, drew a long line with his tongue over the swell of her abdomen, and settled, without warning, between her thighs.

Ruby wanted to come apart right there and then.

His tongue slid over her. Everywhere all at once. From the inside of her thighs to the place where she ached for him most, he was there. Teasing her, taunting her, making her groan with need. Just like he had last time. Just like he was the only man who ever had.

And when she wriggled that little bit too much, he slid his hands beneath her backside, slipping around her bottom and holding her in place whilst he licked into her, hot and deep. He took his time, discovering exactly what made her jolt, what made her moan, and then he set about pleasuring her until she was crying out his name, her hands raking through his hair, not knowing where else to put them.

He learned every inch of her. And then he learned it all over again, making her writhe against him, making her buck her hips, making her arch her back. And just when she thought she couldn't take it anymore, he lowered his mouth and sucked on the very core of her need, sending her spinning off from one burning fire into the next. And each one hotter than the last.

By the time she came back down to earth again, Ivan was naked. As big and thick and perfect as ever, and fresh need juddered through Ruby as she remembered their last time, when she had tasted him. Everywhere. Making him groan in a way that had rumbled right through her entire body. Making her feel more powerful than she had ever felt before—especially in bed.

But this time, it seemed, he had no intention of letting her take charge. Flipping himself onto his back, Ivan hauled her body onto his—giving her the illusion of control though she had no intention of being foolish enough to fall for it. He was like a storm moving over her, through her, and when he used one knee to nudge her legs apart so that he could nestle in between, it was all she could do to obey.

Then, at last, *at last,* he was sliding inside her. Filling her up until she felt utterly possessed. Utterly *his*. And this time there was no stopping herself from screaming his name. Over and over as he hurtled her into space—so high she didn't think she would ever come back down. All she could do was slide her hands around to grab his backside, to pull him into her deeper. Firing them both to the same white-hot finish, and hoping he would catch her when she plummeted back to earth.

And afterwards, Ruby felt happier than she had done in so long—perhaps ever. Everything was a haze of happiness. Euphoria. A surge of emotion welled up within her. Pure, unguarded, almost deliciously overwhelming.

'I love you.'

She didn't realize she'd said the words aloud until she felt Ivan freeze in her arms. Then pull sharply away.

Her hazy brain whirled, trying to replay the last few moments. Had she really said those words out loud?

'That—' Ivan's voice cracked out like thunder '—cannot be.'

'Ivan…'

'I don't do love.' Ivan stood up abruptly, putting

physical distance between them, as if that could somehow insulate him from her declaration.

But she refused to apologize for her feelings. Hadn't she been doing altogether too much of that recently?

'And yet, I love you—' she repeated. Firmer this time.

'I won't allow it,' he said to cut her off, his sharp tone as cold and biting as a blade slicing straight through her.

The precision of a scalpel cut to the heart, wielded with all the skill of a surgeon like Ivan. Ruby fought to brace against the pain, but it was impossible. The warmth that had enveloped her only moments before had turned in an instant into an icy chill.

Worse, the man she had just opened her heart up to was now standing apart from her—perhaps only a few feet literally speaking—but he would clearly wish himself entire worlds away if he could. He was a complete stranger to her.

She pulled the sheet up around herself, feeling suddenly, horribly, shamefully exposed. And not just by the fact that she was naked.

'Ivan—' she tried again, only to be cut off. Again.

'I suggest you think very, *very* carefully about what you say next.'

Sorrow poured through her like heavy, wet concrete. His walls were clearly back up, higher and thicker than ever. Any sign of vulnerability was wholly, irrefutably gone.

'Please, Ivan.' It was a fight with herself not to allow her voice to sound even half as panicked as she felt inside. 'I shouldn't have said that.'

'You are going to tell me that you didn't mean it?' he demanded harshly.

But she couldn't lie. 'No, but I was going to say that you don't need to say it back. Not if you aren't ready yet.'

'Yet?' He stared at her incredulously. 'You think this is something that will change? You're wrong. It won't. And you cannot love me. I will not permit it.'

A lesser woman might have been cowed by the commanding tone.

'This isn't something you can, or cannot, permit,' she pointed out softly. 'Much as you may wish to.'

Ivan fixed her with a look that should have been enough to send chills down her spine. But it didn't. She saw that anger and frustration in his eyes, but there was something else, too. Something deeper. And Ruby thought—hoped—that she knew what it was.

'Then it must end. Right now.'

She eyed him for a moment longer, tilting her head ever so slightly to one side.

'Why?' she asked him softly.

His hands balled into fists at his sides, as if he was fighting some internal battle. No doubt against himself. But his stern expression didn't slip, even for a second.

'You know why,' he rasped. 'This…whatever it is

between us…is not real. It never was. It is nothing more than an agreeable extension of our convenient family for the baby that you are carrying. *My* baby.'

The tension in the room thickened, almost suffocating her with its intensity as Ivan's words demanded an answer. Acquiescence.

But she couldn't oblige. She wouldn't capitulate. Not when she was so certain that he loved her even if he couldn't admit it. Not even to himself. And not when she suspected that Ivan's guilt over his brother was the reason he'd locked away his heart. Refusing to allow himself to be vulnerable.

'It might have started that way.' Her voice sounded louder and clearer than she could have hoped. 'But you and I both know that there is more than that between us. Perhaps there has been from the start.'

'No. I do not accept that.'

'And still, the signs have been there for both of us to see,' she continued gently.

Because the more moments that passed, the more certain she was becoming that his reaction was born more of fear than anything else. That he was trying to shield himself—and possibly her, too—from potential pain.

But it didn't erase the truth in her heart. If anything, it only gave her the courage to continue.

'I love you, Ivan. And I think you love me, too.'

Ivan's jaw clenched visibly, but he didn't move so neither did she. Instead, she watched, waiting and hoping that his cold facade might begin to fissure and crack under the weight of her gaze. A battle of wills between them as they each determined to stand firm to their own truth. Neither of them willing to yield despite the tumultuous emotions patently swirling between them. She could see the conflict raging within him. Surely one of them would have to break eventually.

She might have known, though, that Ivan would never be the one to do so.

'You are mistaken,' Ivan ground out ultimately, when the silence between them had grown so thick she had thought it might crush them both. 'I do not believe in love. I never have. I'm incapable of it.'

'No.' She shook her head, raising herself up onto her knees on the bed, the sheet still wrapped around her. 'I've seen the way you care for your patients. The depth of feeling you have for Vivian. The way your brother knows you loved him.'

'You have no idea what my brother would or would not have felt about me.' Ivan spun away, picking up his discarded jeans first, then his shirt.

'Actually, I do.' The words were tumbling out of her mouth before she could stop them. 'Because he told me.'

The room stilled completely. A vacuum of sound and space. And it might have lasted a second, or it might have lasted entire aeons, until finally, *finally*, Ivan began to turn around.

'What did you say?' he demanded slowly, as if he had trouble articulating every single word.

Ruby swallowed, but forced herself to continue. 'He's alive, Ivan. That neighbour you spoke to *had* helped them to get away. I met with Maksim today.'

That she had made a mistake was instantly evident.

Ivan's reaction was so immediate, so intense, that it sent a chill creeping right down her spine. If the room had felt cold before, it was nothing compared to the subzero chill that filled it now. Ivan's eyes hardened, darkening to the blackest onyx. His jaw so tight that she was afraid it might actually shatter.

'My brother is alive?' he bit out, as if every syllable was glass in his mouth. 'And he was here?'

'No… I thought it best to meet away from here so when I said I was in town, I drove a couple of hours south.' She paused for a moment, trying to gauge his reaction. 'I thought it was best until I knew what Maksim thought.'

'*You* thought it was best?' Ivan asked far too quietly for Ruby's liking.

'Yes, I…' Ruby's voice petered out.

All she'd wanted to do was help Ivan, but it was patently obvious just how seriously she had misjudged the situation.

Yet still, she couldn't bring herself to feign ignorance. There was too much pain in Ivan, and until he dealt with it, she was terribly afraid that there could be no real future for them as a family. She owed him this much. And, Ruby thought as she cradled her belly, she owed it to their unborn child.

'Ivan, just because you lock the past away in a box and bury it, it doesn't mean it's gone. It only means you're denying its existence.'

'It's gone for me,' he bit out harshly. 'Over. Done with.'

His words were a shield against the truth that seemed to haunt the room, and Ruby's heart clenched painfully at the sound of them. He looked so distant, so guarded—a man so utterly besieged by ghosts that she couldn't even begin to see.

'Except that it isn't,' she whispered. 'Not when I know you keep that old fairground photograph in your apartment. And not when you can't even hear me tell you I love you.'

'Stop saying that,' he barked, and her chest cracked open at the expressions of pain that snatched at his impossibly handsome features.

'Why?' she pressed quietly. 'Because it might make you feel something?'

The growl he emitted was almost animalistic.

'No,' he snapped and gritted his teeth. 'Because I don't want to hear it. I don't believe in it. Love isn't real—it's nothing more than a dangerous lie. It gets people hurt.'

Yet the words seemed to cost him more than he was prepared to pay. Turning abruptly away, Ivan moved away from her and into the shadows that danced at the edges of the soft night light. Like Hades moving towards the darker underworld.

Ruby watched the rigid line of Ivan's back, the bare muscles of his back taut with an anguish he refused to let her see as he stared out the window into the night.

'Don't you even want to know what he said?' she ventured, after what felt like an eternity.

'I do not.'

Except that he didn't try to shut her down. He didn't even move.

'He has had a good life, Ivan,' she told him simply. 'Not straight away, but pretty quickly.'

'I do not wish to hear,' Ivan growled—possibly at her but more likely at his own reflection.

'His mother fled the night the old woman said. Maksim said she dragged him from one village to another, begging, borrowing, stealing, but never staying in the same place for long.'

'I do not care,' he bit out when she paused for breath.

But Ruby ignored him. 'This story is Maksim's to tell rather than mine, but whilst you're too scared to face him, I'll have to give you the bare bones.'

'Do not bother.'

'Too late.' Ruby feigned nonchalance. 'So, for the first month or so, she actually managed to look after him better than might have been expected, but after that she fell back into old habits. This time, however, a neighbour saw and they stepped in. Maksim ended up in a home, but he got lucky and the long-term foster placement he was given turned out to be a perfect fit. They fostered him for five years, and then adopted him as soon as they were able.'

'Sounds like a fairy-tale ending,' he drawled, his tone suggesting different.

And anyone else might have been fooled, but Ruby wasn't. This was classic Ivan, concealing his hurt, his scars, with indifference and distance.

'They loved Maksim, and he loved them. A *fairy-tale ending* doesn't sound like it's too far off the mark,' she agreed brightly. 'And you did that, Ivan.'

She'd hoped Ivan would be relieved. Proud. Even happy. But Ruby quickly realized that she'd underestimated that, too.

'Don't you see, Ivan?' she prompted softly when he still didn't answer. 'You saved Maksim. Just as you'd set out to do.'

'I seriously doubt that,' Ivan spat out, making her blink in surprise.

Her heart picked up its pace. Clearly, he hadn't heard what she'd said. He hadn't had the chance to process it.

'What isn't in doubt, however,' he continued furiously as he finally spun back around, 'is that you crossed a line by tracking down my brother. Worse, by contacting him.'

'I wanted to help you,' she cried. 'You must see that.'

'I've kept my past buried for a reason.' Ivan ignored her cry, his frustration and fury growing by the second. 'You had absolutely no right to go digging it all up.'

And all she wanted to do was hurry over to him and throw her arms around him, the way she knew he needed her to do. The way he was so desperate for someone to do.

But deep down, she knew he wouldn't thank her for it. Not now. He still wasn't ready to let go of the past and move on. Yet the more she tried to gently nudge him forward, the more she was clearly pushing him away.

And still, she had to keep trying.

'A past that you've buried because not knowing was too horrifying,' she pointed out. It was not an accusation so much as a plea for him to consider alternative outcomes. 'And that's stopping you from really opening your heart to love.'

'Perhaps so,' Ivan managed harshly, his control slipping as his voice rose. 'But love doesn't erase fear, Ruby. Nor does it fix broken families or mend years of torment.'

'What if love gives us strength to face those fears? To start to heal what has been damaged? You could just try, Ivan. Just meet your brother. Hear whatever he has to say. At least you'll know.'

'No, I cannot.' Ivan shook his head, a maelstrom of emotion swirling behind his eyes. 'I won't. It's too much of a risk. It's over and done, Ruby. If what you say is true, then Maksim and I have our own lives now and they are completely separate from each other. That's how they need to stay.'

And she could let it go right there and then. But how could she when her heart grieved so dreadfully for him? Just as Ivan mourned the brother he'd lost in trying to save him.

'Whatever you think, Maksim is a part of you, whether you want to admit it or not.' She desperately scanned his face for any sign that she was reaching him. 'He's a vital part of your past, and I'm terribly afraid that until you make him a part of your future—or at least your present—then you can never put the past to rest.'

'You have no idea,' Ivan spat out, no longer able to contain his anger. 'And you had no damned right to contact him.'

'I just thought…'

'No, you didn't.' He stalked across the room, buttoning up his paint-soiled shirt with such force that it was amazing it didn't shred right in his hands. 'You didn't think at all. You knew I had chosen not to search for Maksim, but you did it anyway.'

'To help,' she pleaded, but his face was as hard and implacable as his icy tone.

'I trusted you, and you betrayed me,' he told her. 'And I can never forgive you for that.'

'Ivan…'

'I'll support my child, and this house is yours as long as you want it. But this…' He gestured between them, a gulf that suddenly seemed impossible to bridge. '*Us.* It was a mistake. We cannot be a part of each other's lives.'

Her heart splintered at his words, so violently that she half expected the room to be showered in its fractured shards.

'You don't mean that,' she gasped, scarcely able to breathe.

'Believe whatever you want to,' he clipped out. 'I no longer care.'

And then, as she sat on the bed scrambling for something—anything—to say to stop him, he yanked open the door so that it swung violently on its hinges, and strode out.

Leaving Ruby alone in a room that felt like it was closing in on her with every passing second. The sound of her ragged breathing reached her ears but she was helpless to silence herself. The future that she had begun to imagine—full of hope, and promise, and *love*—now lay shattered at her feet.

In so many tattered pieces that there was no hope of ever patching it back together again.

CHAPTER THIRTEEN

FINISHING METICULOUSLY SCRUBBING IN, Ivan carefully fitted his mask over his face and inhaled with relief as he stepped through the doors of his operating room in his private London clinic.

This place had been his sanctuary these past couple of weeks. Sixteen painful days, to be exact. He knew it down to the hour, and the operating room had been his haven in all that time, his escape from the turmoil that had been chasing through him every moment since Ruby had no longer been a part of his life.

Out there, in the real world, he couldn't seem to push back down the strange mix of emotions that she had brought bubbling to the surface with her efforts to get him to reconnect with his estranged brother. And the unfamiliar, unwanted, and most of all deeply unsettling emotions churned through him, over and over, whether he was working in his office, cooking a meal, or pounding the parklands for mile after mile after mile.

But his OR was his fortress of concentration. In here, it was all about the patient, the surgery; there was no room for any other thoughts. And somehow, that offered him much-needed peace. Four simple walls which somehow created a powerful haven from the jumble of sentiments. The place where his years of dedication, and honing his skills, were all that mattered. Where his surgical precision and instinct were all that counted. No self-recriminations. No second-guessing. Every second in here was carved into the fabric of fate, yet it all felt second nature to him.

Unlike the complexities of sharing his life with Ruby.

Thrusting the unwanted thoughts from his head, Ivan focused on the imminent surgery—an abraded punch graft procedure.

Carefully, he dermabraded the area before correcting the pitted facial scars. It was a slow and meticulous task which demanded his concentration and left no room for any other, unwanted thoughts.

Of anyone.

Though it seemed all too ironic that the marks on his patient's face were nothing to the scars he knew Ruby carried in her heart. Something he wouldn't have been so sensitive to a matter of months ago.

Now she almost reminded him of himself, and he wielded his scalpel like a sword against the memories and doubts that would threaten to slay him. And he wouldn't ever admit to anyone that there was a secret part of him that wondered as he carefully punched, abraded, and sutured—healing the damaged skin and making it appear whole again—if perhaps one day, he could find a way to also heal the fragments of his own fractured world.

As he worked, slowly and methodically, the edges of Ivan's vision tunnelled, the bright overhead lights casting an unforgiving glare on the exposed tissues before him whilst the rhythmic beeping of the heart monitor kept a low, monotonous beat as they counted the seconds, then the minutes, and finally the hours.

At last the surgery was complete and his focus was over—and even before he had finished scrubbing out, the real world started to instantly press on the edges of Ivan's mind.

Like wondering how Ruby and the baby were doing, given that Ruby was officially approaching her third trimester.

And then he told himself that the frisson that just rippled through him at the realization was nothing more than medical curiosity rather than a surge of unexpected emotion.

At twenty-one weeks their baby would be developing essential skills like sucking and breathing, it would be evolving its sense of taste, and it would be establishing its waking patterns, which could well be when Ruby was trying to sleep.

He hoped she wasn't feeling overwhelmed with the changes her body had to be going through.

Was she taking care of herself? Getting enough sleep?

Ivan berated himself. It was not his business to tell her what to do, yet he couldn't shake the feeling of concern for her well-being, and as he changed out of his surgical scrubs and into his daily clothes, the weight of his thoughts about Ruby and the baby settled heavier on his shoulders.

With each step he took back to his office—away from his operating room sanctuary—the more he felt the pull of his personal life growing stronger, tugging at the edges of his carefully compartmentalized mind.

His footsteps grew heavier as he made his way back to his office and thought of the cold emptiness of it. What wouldn't he give for a coffee at *Re-cuperation,* or to hear Ruby's gentle laugh that whatever the vending machines at City Hospital spewed out, it wasn't *coffee*?

Throwing open his office door, Ivan thrust the memories from his thoughts and faced the stack of paperwork on his desk and the flashing lights on his phone that indicated a couple of messages. With a sigh, he sank down heavily into his chair and played the first one. He was about to move onto the second when it lit up with an interruption from his receptionist.

He answered it quickly, and there was a nervous clearing of the throat on the other end.

'There's a visitor for you in reception, Dr Volkov.'

Ruby?

He schooled himself not to react. To quash that flash of hope that he suspected had been about to penetrate his chest. Because what good would it do for them to speak again? What had changed in the past couple of weeks?

Was it only that long? It felt like an eternity, perhaps two.

And the simple truth was that nothing had changed. *Nothing.*

Because she had still betrayed him, contacting Maksim—*meeting* him. And Ivan had nothing more to offer her than he had two weeks ago. He was still the same broken, wrecked man he had been then. Being a surgeon was his only saving grace—it was the only thing he should be focused on from now on.

'Advise her that I will be indisposed until late into the evening.'

And no matter that he hated the sound of each word that came out of his mouth. Almost as much as he hated himself for saying it.

The line crackled and Ivan braced himself for his instruction to be acknowledged. He certainly wasn't expecting his receptionist to counter him.

'It isn't a *she*.' The hesitation in the voice was unmistakable. 'It's a man and he says he's your brother.'

Something jagged and exacting shot through Ivan in that instant.

'Maksim?' Ivan wasn't aware he'd uttered the name aloud until it was confirmed by the voice over the intercom.

'He says he'll wait as long as it takes.'

Time seemed to freeze. His mind first went utterly blank, then was filled with so many half-finished thoughts that Ivan didn't know where to start. And all of it happened within a fraction of a second.

Conflicting emotions charged around his brain as he gritted his teeth so tightly that he was half-afraid his jaw might shatter. It took Ivan longer than it should have to push aside the doubts that momentarily haunted the edges of his mind at the revelation that the unexpected visitor was Maksim of all people. But there was something else, too. Something Ivan hadn't been able to eject even though he tried.

That traitorous hint of hope. And the realization that Ruby had been right to contact his brother after all. No matter everything he'd told himself about keeping his distance and letting the past lie buried, the realization that Maksim was here, *now*, filled Ivan with an undeniably fierce need to hasten down the corridor and look at his baby brother with his own eyes.

To understand what had happened.

And suddenly, it became too clear to Ivan that it was the *not knowing* that had chewed him up inside, far more than anything Maksim could have to tell him. However his little brother judged him for that fateful decision two decades ago, whatever kind of life Maksim had endured—it was better to know than to fear the worst.

Before he knew what he was doing, Ivan found

himself out of his seat and halfway out of the room, marching briskly as he navigated the warren of corridors with renewed purpose. Because even if Maksim hated him for his choices, Ruby was right to have pushed him to confront them. She hadn't been wrong when she'd urged him that it was better to face his demons than to hide from them any longer.

She hadn't been betraying him; she'd been trying to set him free. So why the hell had it taken this long to see it?

Ruby. She'd understood the weight of his past choices bearing down on him, threatening to crush him, far better than he ever had. She'd cared enough to want to help him find a way out from under it. And he'd thanked her by accusing her of betraying him—by leaving her to deal with the pregnancy all alone.

He'd let her down the way he'd let Maksim down—precisely the opposite of the very man he'd wanted to be.

Right there he made a vow that the moment he had spoken with his brother—no matter if Maksim hated him, or had come to terms with what he'd done back then—he would return directly to Little Meadwood and find Ruby. Perhaps not to make things right, since it was too late for that, but to apologize for what he'd said and to thank her for the courage and wisdom that she'd clearly shown.

But first, he had to get through this—and even

as he approached the reception area, Ivan couldn't prevent his pulse from speeding up. From anxiety settling in every bone of his body. What would his brother say to him? What was he even to begin to say to Maksim? Would they even know each other?

For a moment, he wished Ruby was with him. One look in those warm, hazel eyes that always seemed such a balm to the tempest within him—even when she was mad with him. Her mouth that could curve up in a way that her smile was as glorious as the dawn breaking through the darkness. Her touch that seemed so gentle yet fired him up in a way no woman had ever done before.

Ivan felt a smile play on his lips at the memory as he paused, temporarily frozen, on the other side of the reception doors. Ruby was the only person who had made him feel everything—and nothing—all at once. So alive, yet burden free. And he had pushed her away. What kind of a pathetic man did that make him?

The kind who knew he couldn't give her what she needed, a voice needled inside his head, reminding him of facts he would do well not to forget again.

Ruby deserved better than he could ever offer her.

So, wiping the foolish smile away, Ivan thrust out his hands to the heavy oak and strode across the threshold.

Then stopped dead.

Maksim.

Even if he hadn't known his estranged brother was waiting in that room, he would have recognized the man who rose instantly to his feet from the waiting room couch. Gone was the scrawny kid that Ivan remembered, and in his place a man who felt so familiar that it was almost like looking in the mirror.

Yet somehow there was an easiness about Maksim that Ivan didn't recognize. A softer side, as though he hadn't been worn down by life's harshest strokes, the way that he himself had been. Or was that just his subconscious, wanting to believe what Ruby had said about Maksim's childhood having turned out far better than much of his own?

The unfamiliar sensation of uncertainty threaded its way through Ivan much like his shared history with his brother—a tapestry woven with pain, resilience, and the violence they'd never spoken about even as kids. Not until he'd shared a glimpse of it with Ruby. Did Maksim have someone in his life like that?

Ivan had no idea how long he stood there, rooted in place and staring at the familiar stranger who wasn't moving or speaking, either. Did he, too, sense the past that loomed between them, tangible and disquieting?

'Maksim,' Ivan uttered at length, his usually commanding voice faltering and betraying his surprise.

The other man's tentative smile did little to mask

the apprehension in his dark eyes—eyes so like Ivan's own but with flecks that were lacking when Ivan looked in a mirror. How had he forgotten that detail about his little brother?

Yet he wasn't convinced it was merely the almost-identical colour which was so unsettling. Ivan couldn't shake the sense that this other man's eyes reflected a world he had fought hard to leave behind. A world that he had convinced himself he actually *had* left behind.

But now the memories were creeping back. Unkind and unwelcome, leaving Ivan struggling to suck in a breath and feeling winded—as though his father was right there in front of him, ready to beat him as he always had. It was only Maksim's voice which dragged Ivan back into the present.

'Hello, brother,' Maksim spoke with a careful neutrality. 'It has been a long time.'

For a second, Ivan wasn't certain he would be able to reply. He moved his vocal cords up and down, as if unsure his mouth would cooperate.

'It has,' Ivan managed a reply at last, though the words felt foreign on his lips.

'Yes.'

Another long silence, and Ivan resisted the sudden urge to move his weight from one foot to the other, the polished granite floor suddenly felt like shifting sands beneath him. If that wasn't enough, the charged silence jolted through his body, shaking

Ivan to his core and awakening even more ghosts of memories that now demanded to be heard.

Everything suddenly felt too bright, too sharp, too stark. But it was too late to slam the lid back on that proverbial box. Too late to walk away. Especially when—the longer they stood there—the more the stream of unwanted memories became a deluge, threatening to break through the dam that was his composure.

Not just memories of beatings, but memories of a cold so biting that it might as well have taken their fingers off; a hunger so excruciating that he could happily have hollowed out his own stomach with the bluntest of knives.

But abruptly—unexpectedly—among those painful memories, Ivan caught a few surprise snatched moments of happiness. That forgotten closeness that he and Maksim had once shared. The weeks they had been okay, just the two of them, when their father had been away from home on some bender or other, and Maksim's mother had been too out of it to help. The vow he'd made to protect little Maksim against their father's wrath, and the pride he'd felt at succeeding.

Which only made it all the more painful to reflect on how they had ended up here. No longer boys, but men—no longer brothers, but strangers. Bound by blood yet separated by a chasm filled with years and unsaid truths. But none of them to be voiced here in reception, in front of too many sets of prying ears.

'Come through,' Ivan clipped out curtly, pulling himself together at last. 'We can speak in my office.'

As his younger brother offered a terse dip of his head, Ivan spun around and led the way back down the high-gloss corridors and to the door marked with his name. His brother was keeping pace with him, yet neither of them closing the gap at all on the other.

Even when Ivan pushed open the door, he walked in first, leaving Maksim to follow at a considered distance. Then, as if by unspoken agreement, the two men claimed chairs on opposite sides of the desk, as though each was taking comfort from the physical distance. Then, once again, the quiet pressed in on them.

'I can't believe that you are here, Maksim.' Ivan forced himself to break the silence, though he feared the wariness that laced his voice also belied his attempt to show that he was in control of his emotions.

Although if his brother noticed then he didn't show it.

'Ruby found me.' Maksim fixed Ivan's gaze with a direct stare of his own. 'She related to me the story you'd told her. I realized it was time we spoke.'

'Up until a few minutes ago I would have said

that she should not have done that,' Ivan growled. 'I had no intention of intruding on your life.'

'That was made clear to me.'

And though Ivan scrutinised the words for what Maksim wasn't saying, the tension in the room seemed to be thickening with every passing second yet he felt powerless to prevent it. His brother's expression remained frustratingly neutral, a mask that revealed none of his true feelings.

Ivan pressed on anyway.

'However the moment my receptionist told me you were here, I realized that it has been the not-knowing that has bound me all these years. Even if you hate me, I am grateful that Ruby did what she did.'

'Ruby does not seem like the kind of woman who seeks permission for things she believes to be right,' a soft smile played around Maksim's lips, startling Ivan momentarily. 'Or am I wrong, brother?'

Any further disapproval Ivan might have been ready to make evaporated in an instant. All he could focus on was how the word 'brother' hung in the air between them. A relic from a past Ivan had never thought he'd hear again. A name he'd long-since compartmentalized and sealed away.

Brother.

He wanted to leap up and clasp Maksim in the embrace he once used to do, and never let go. Ivan's fists grasped the arms of his chair as he kept himself absolutely still.

'How is she?' his brother asked suddenly. 'And the baby?'

'Ruby and I are no longer together,' Ivan admitted, not realizing he'd been about to utter the words until he heard them spilling from his mouth.

Too much information. But it was too late to swallow them back now.

Maksim, however, narrowed his eyes shrewdly.

'Oh?' There was that irritatingly calm demeanour again. 'That is a shame. Not everyone finds that person who will fight for them the way she did for you. The way that you did for me.'

Ivan tried to stop his jaw from clenching, but he couldn't. That ache around his chest tightened further as he stared at his brother. What was he to say? Or think? There were too many emotions crowding inside him, pulling him in different directions, threatening to rip him apart.

'I'm ashamed to say it took me far too long to realize that,' Ivan manged simply. 'But now I have, I intend to remedy it as soon as possible.'

How was it he was confessing things to his brother that he would never have confessed to anyone else? As if they had never been apart?

It had to be Ruby's influence—another thing to be grateful to her for.

'I'm glad,' Maksim noted after a pause. 'She seemed like quite a remarkable woman. But I did not come here to lecture you on your life. I did come here to talk about you and I. About our past.'

Despite the neutrality of his tone, his younger brother leaned forward as though psychologically wanting to bridge some of the distance between them. But though Ivan realized he wanted to do the same, he found it impossible to move.

It only made it all the clearer to Ivan that although Ruby had already helped him to soften so much, he still had a long way to go. But for the first time, he knew that he wanted to. He had spent years crafting his environment, his world, to ensure that nothing reached him, but he no longer wanted to be so remote, so detached, so isolated.

And that was all thanks to Ruby.

'I would like that,' he managed to answer his brother at last.

And for a moment they merely sat in silence. But far from being an awkward one, it gave them both chance to regroup.

'The truth is,' Maksim began, and this time Ivan was gratified to hear the crack in his brother's voice which suggested the younger man wasn't as in control as he appeared, 'I owe you more than you know. You shielded me from the worst of what happened in that house. You fed me, washed me, clothed me. How many nights did you go hungry just so that I wouldn't have to?'

'I was the older brother.'

'You were my brother, my father, my mother, all rolled into one,' Maksim countered. 'I don't think I would have survived if not for you.'

'It was my job to protect you.'

'And whose job was it to protect *you*?'

As his brother's words found their mark, Ivan felt his breath catching in his chest. His defences, so carefully constructed, began to erode.

He suspected Ruby had already played her part in softening them, too.

'That isn't how it works…' he choked out, unable to bear looking at his brother.

How could he, when the image reflected back at him was not one of a hardened survivor, scarred and bitter, but rather a guardian whose love had been fierce and unwavering? It wasn't right. It wasn't accurate. It wasn't who he'd been.

Yet his brother seemed to disagree.

'You were there for me every single day,' Maksim ground out. 'You saved me and I let you down.'

'Stop.' Ivan barked out the single-word command like a reflex honed from years in the operating room. 'You make me out to be something I was not. I was trying to survive, but I didn't save you. If I had, then I never would have left you.'

'If you hadn't got out, he would have killed you,' Maksim spoke quietly but there was no denying the thickness in his voice. 'We both know that.'

'But in doing so, I left you there with him,' Ivan choked out as he thrust back his chair and stood, too pent-up to stay seated any longer.

'You had no choice.' Maksim shrugged. 'And

you did what you said. The authorities got there that night.'

Fury spread through Ivan. 'And they did nothing. They ignored your bruises, they believed his lies, and they left. I let you down.'

'You frightened them,' his brother pointed out. 'Enough that he didn't come near us for a week. By then, my mother had planned her escape. We left in the middle of the night.'

'Because I failed you.'

'You didn't fail me,' Maksim refuted, pulling something out of his pocket. 'You were my hero, Ivan. Always.'

'I ripped our family apart,' Ivan growled, and though he fought not to, his voice broke as his self-control crumbled. 'I *left* you with them. I should never have done that.'

He turned his back to his brother, caught off guard when Maksim slid something across his desk. An old photo, much like the one he himself had kept, except with slightly different poses.

'Do you remember this, Ivan? Do you remember the pact we made to always protect each other?'

His hands shaking uncharacteristically, Ivan placed his fingers on the photo and pulled it to him. His eyes raked over the fairground picture slowly, absorbing every familiar detail.

But whilst in his photo the two of them were on a horse merry-go-round, in Maksim's they'd been dunking for apples and were both soaked.

'I remember,' he rasped, his voice cracking.

'Well, you did that, Ivan. You saved my life,' Maksim said quietly. 'Many times, but especially that night. You risked everything and I let you.'

His brother's words echoed in the room, louder than the most deafening of silences. The words were swirling in the air around them, settling on him, threatening to exploit any crack they could find in the high walls Ivan had spent years building for himself.

Walls that he suspected Ruby had already begun to weaken from their very foundations.

'I looked for you, you know,' he admitted at last. 'I returned to that house, but you weren't there.'

'Ruby told me.'

Ivan took a breath. 'I didn't know if he'd done something to you. No one would tell me.'

'Most didn't know. Only old lady Craven—she took our bags and hid them until we were ready to go.'

'I asked her, too,' Ivan ground out. 'She eventually told me you both left in the middle of one night. But I never knew whether to believe her or whether that was just what my father had told her.'

'You did everything you could possibly have done,' Maksim confirmed. 'You were there for me, but I should have been there for you, too. I should have told someone—anyone—what was happening. I should have protected you, too.'

A swell of emotions threatened to undo Ivan.

Pride, regret, and an ache for the bond they once shared—all intertwined.

'How could you have protected me? You were a kid.' Ivan shook his head, the very idea being too much for him.

But it seemed that was his brother's point.

'I could have looked for you the way you looked for me. I could have told my adopted family that I had a brother. I left you alone, Ivan. And I'm more sorry than you will ever know.'

'That isn't necessary,' Ivan murmured, but a fissure was forming in the walls around his heart, and if he wasn't careful, he was rather afraid it might blow those walls out.

'Maybe not for you,' Maxim insisted gently. 'But for me, it is.'

Ivan shook his head, struggling to take it all in. And as the two brothers sat there, their shared dark history finally beginning to dissipate now that it had finally been aired in the bright light of day, something cracked deep inside Ivan and everything simply...*shifted.*

'I never expected to see you again, Maksim,' he confessed, his voice low and sincere. 'Let alone for you to forgive me.'

For a moment, the younger man merely stared at him before replying, 'You misunderstand, big brother. There is nothing to forgive.'

And that simply, that easily, the crushing weight of years of self-recrimination, loathing, and guilt seemed to just seep out of Ivan's chest. With it, he could feel the weight of his childhood lighten ever so slightly—the acknowledgement from Maxim acting as a balm to old wounds that he had never even known he needed.

But Ruby had known. And she had done the one thing that he himself could never have managed. If not for her conviction that meeting Maksim was the closure he needed on his past—the turning point for him to finally move on with his future, and with their child that she was carrying—he would still be caged up inside that prison of his own making.

She had known what he needed when he himself had railed against it. And she had fought for him in spite of his ire.

No matter how much he tried to tell himself that he didn't care about this crazy, funny, unique woman, Ivan knew it was a lie. Perhaps it had always been a lie. And now these feelings, this...*tenderness* pushed inside him—tentative but growing all the same, like the first hopeful sprouts pushing through the cracks of a long-frozen earth.

A fondness—more than fondness—for Ruby, a woman whose kindness was innate and who saw beyond his guarded exterior to the vulnerability he had never dared to expose. And he should loathe her for doing so. But he didn't. He couldn't. He loved her.

He loved her.

For the first time in his life, Ivan felt the floodgates of his heart begin to buckle. A tentative drip at first, and then a trickle. Before long, it would be a river and then a torrent of emotions that he had kept tightly sealed for far, far too long.

He was in love with Ruby, and though he and Maksim had more—so much more—to discuss, once that was done, he knew the first thing he needed to do would be to find Ruby. And to tell her how she'd also been right about the way he felt about her.

He loved her. And he loved their unborn baby.

It was finally time to stop hiding from himself, and to claim his family.

CHAPTER FOURTEEN

Ruby was smoothing down her favourite steampunk outfit at Nell's stall for the village fête—waiting for her friend to finish talking to an eager couple who were clearly trying to decide which costumes to choose—when she sensed Ivan behind her, moments before he spoke.

'Ruby.'

Uncertain if she'd imagined it, she turned. Slowly. As though she was afraid that if she spun around too fast it would cause him to disappear.

But when she finished her agonizing pivot, he was still there. In the flesh.

'Ivan,' she began, hating herself for the way she seemed to just drink him in—head to toe—unable to help herself.

But something hitched inside as she realized something was…*different. He* was different. And she didn't need him to tell her that he'd finally spoken with his brother. It was etched into every ridge on his impossibly handsome face. Given away by that sudden…*lightness* to him, as if a huge burden had been lifted from his shoulders. Even the darkness of his eyes somehow held a glint that showed he was…*happier.*

And even though she knew he would never forgive her for betraying his trust, it brought her relief to know that what she'd done hadn't been a total loss. Even so, she was shocked when he started to speak.

'You were right,' he stated, his voice raspier than she had expected.

Ruby blinked, unsure what she was supposed to say. 'Okay,' she managed weakly, at last.

'About Maksim. About me.' He took another step towards her, then stopped. 'About everything.'

He was breathing as hard as if he'd just run a race, though it was clear he had done no such thing, and whatever she'd hoped for in those secret dreams in the darkest hours of the night, it hadn't been this. Ivan Volkov, the Prince of Guarded Emotions, standing in front of her, vulnerable and open. The heady rush of emotions almost left her breathless.

The words hung in the air between them, his raw honesty taking her utterly by surprise. After all that had been said between them—or hadn't—this might have been enough for her. But it seemed Ivan had more to say.

'Can we talk?'

His voice was low but sure. Determined. Not that she had any desire to refuse him. Not when she'd spent so long willing him to open up to her. Even a little bit. All the same, Ruby had no idea how she managed to keep her tone so calm and even.

'Of course.'

With a brief glance over her shoulder to see Nell

still absorbed in conversation with the young couple, Ruby gave Ivan a slight nod and followed him out of the stall and across the bustling village green.

'You were right about Maksim having had a good life,' Ivan told her once they'd walked the length of the cricket pitch.

Again Ruby nodded, but it was the sheer relief in Ivan's tone that tugged at something deep within her. The release from the blame that he'd placed on himself all these years. And as she walked beside him on the quiet path that ran down from the green to the abandoned railway line, she couldn't help noticing the subtle changes in him. Even his gait seemed somehow less…laden with duty.

Was it just her imagination, or was she sensing that familiar connection building between them—only better? As though Ivan was no longer fighting to keep his distance? To shut her out?

Ruby fought to control the flare of hope that went off inside her chest.

As they reached a secluded bench under a canopy of trees next to the abandoned Victorian railway line—its tracks long gone with only the cinder path the remaining witness to the line's heyday—Ivan sank down almost gratefully and stared off into the distance before retrieving something from his pocket which he placed in Ruby's palms. And his hands, usually so rock-steady when wielding a scalpel, trembled faintly as he traced the outline of the old fairground photograph that Maksim had handed him.

The edges were worn, and the colours were faded, but there was no mistaking the image of two young boys with tentative smiles—a bond that had been both a lifeline and a source of infinite pain.

'Maksim kept this,' Ivan murmured, his voice barely above a whisper, the sound swallowed by the hum of the village fête around them. 'He said it reminded him of our promise, our pact to always look out for each other.'

He handed it to her and she took it carefully.

'That's like the photograph in your London apartment,' Ruby murmured, love blooming all the brighter inside her.

Except that Ivan didn't want her love. He didn't want anything from her at all.

Then why is he here?

The voice whispered in her head before she could silence it, so instead she pretended not to hear it. She focused on the unmistakable battle in Ivan's eyes—evidence of a war waged within his own head, between regret and acceptance.

'I was wrong to say you had betrayed me,' Ivan continued, lifting his gaze to meet Ruby's. 'I was wrong to blame you. All those years, I carried the guilt of my separation from Maksim, and I didn't want to face it. It was easier to be angry at you for raising the past than it was for me to actually confront my own missteps.

'Maksim never blamed you, did he?' Ruby couldn't help herself from asking. Gently, without condemnation. A feather-light touch that urged Ivan to finally unfurl the truth that was clenched so tightly in his fist.

He exhaled heavily, a breath that seemed to carry years of misgivings with it.

'No, he never blamed me. How brave he had to have been, left alone with them.'

'Bravery doesn't always wear a medal, Ivan.' She shook her head gently, reaching out to return the photo to him so that he could look at it again. 'Sometimes it's in the choices we make, the ones that change the course of our lives. You and your brother made a pact to protect each other, and that was what you did—just perhaps not in the way you had expected to. Your courage wasn't in fists or force. It was in your voice, your willingness to shatter the silence that traps so many others.'

'He told me that he forgave me,' he rasped at length. 'Actually, that isn't true—he told me that there was nothing to forgive.'

'From the conversation I had with your brother,' Ruby offered tentatively, 'I think he's right.'

'He isn't.' Without warning, Ivan reached his hand out; his long fingers stroked her cheek just once, but it was enough to make her almost feverish.

'I need to know if you can forgive me,' he rasped. 'I treated you badly, telling you that you had betrayed me—even *believing* that you would have done so. I was scared, and racked with guilt, and I took it out on you.'

'You didn't trust me,' Ruby managed, her throat thick with emotion. 'You wouldn't even hear me out.'

'And that was my mistake. But one, I swear to you, that I will never make again. I should have believed in you, Ruby, the way you always believed in me.'

She almost forgot how to breathe.

'Yes,' she choked out.

'Why did you believe in me?'

She hesitated. The answer was so complex yet simultaneously so straightforward.

'Because the teenage boy I knew all those years ago, back at Vivian's, was kind and compassionate. I could never stand to see the way you seemed to hate yourself. I thought you were worth far more.'

She stopped as the words hung in the hot summer air. The quiet rustle of the leaves and distant murmur of the village fête stopped the silence from becoming too heavy.

'I was broken, Ruby.' His voice was low, but no less charged with emotion. 'I was terrified of becoming *him*, my father, and passing on that cruel streak. And his selfishness.'

Ruby's hand tentatively found its way to his, her touch light but anchoring.

'You are not your father, Ivan. You have a kind

heart. I see it every day in how you care for your patients, for me, for our unborn baby.'

'I want to believe that.' Ivan swallowed hard, the muscles in his jaw tightening. 'I've been so afraid of the darkness in me, of the legacy I might pass on…but my brother showed me another side to myself that I had never allowed myself to see before. The side that you've been trying to show me all this time. I'm sorry I didn't listen to you.'

'I understand why you needed Maksim to be the one to make you see it,' Ruby assured him. As though her chest wasn't swelling with all the emotions she was trying to keep in.

'I want to be a father, Ruby,' Ivan announced suddenly. 'Not like him—never like him—but someone who is present, caring…loving. Someone our child can depend on.'

'I know that. I've always known it.'

'Well, I want to do that with you.' Ivan's eyes were earnest, reflecting the clear blue sky above them. 'I want us to build a life that's ours, filled with love and not the shadows of either of our pasts.'

Ruby's breath caught in her throat as she absorbed his words. Could it really be that her own dreams of a real family were finally coming to life right in front of her? But this was no fantasy, dreamed of in the middle of night when her mother was in hospital and her foster mother was asleep. This was potentially real, with all the complexities and scars they both carried.

'I want that, too,' she managed, barely recognizing her own voice.

'But do you really believe we could have a future together that is untainted by the past? Pure?'

'I do,' she assured him solemnly. 'Love is not a force to be wielded, Ivan, but a gift to be offered without strings.'

'Then I am offering my love to you.'

'Before you do, you should know that I have a confession of my own to make,' Ruby began, licking her lips as she searched for the right words. 'These past few weeks have made me wonder if that picture-perfect vision I had of a future family—of a life together—might not be quite realistic.'

'Oh?'

She could practically see the shutters begin to drop in his expression and before she could stop herself, Ruby shot her hand out to touch his chest.

The contact was electric. Her hand splayed, palm down as if drawing energy from the contact.

'And I think that's a good thing,' she stumbled on, still searching for the right words. 'I think I needed to let go of those naive, childlike expectations. The perfect life that I used to pretend I had when I was a kid. Like being a princess and living in a castle.'

'I'm not a prince,' Ivan told her gravely. 'And I don't have a castle.'

'That's my point.' She lifted her eyes to meet

his. 'It might have taken me a while to grow out of that fantasy—my comfort blanket from being in and out of foster care—but I'm finally realizing that I don't need either. I just need someone who will stand with me through life's storms. No matter how fierce they may get.'

And it was true. Gone were those girlish daydreams of white picket fences and storybook endings. Life wasn't like that. It was messier, more complicated, and filled with give and take. Just as Vivian had always tried to teach her.

Life with someone you loved meant finding a balance. And Ruby wanted that balance with Ivan Volkov, more than she ever could have imagined.

'And what if sometimes *I* am the storm?' Ivan rasped, a tormented expression momentarily clouding his eyes.

'Then I'll be your anchor,' she declared and pressed her hand harder to his chest. 'Besides, sometimes a storm is exactly what is needed to bring a new, brighter dawn.'

'I believe you will.' Ivan's eyes softened as he gazed at her. 'And I vow to spend every second of every day loving you for it. And making sure you never regret that decision.'

And the smile that touched Ruby's lips flooded up from deep inside her. The weight of his words and depth of his commitment to her washed over like the softest of embraces on a hot summer day.

It was only when he slid off the wooden bench and onto one knee on the grass before her that she realized what he really meant.

'Ruby, there's something I need to ask you.'

As her breath hitched, exhilaration pulsed through her and her gaze dropped of its own volition to Ivan's upturned palm. A sapphire-and-diamond ring sat nestled on the most velvety blue cushion.

'Be my wife, Ruby?' Ivan's voice cracked with vulnerability she didn't think she'd ever heard before. 'Not out of duty, and not because of the precious baby that you are carrying, but because we love each other. Because together, we can overcome any challenge that comes our way.'

And Ruby wasn't sure it was only her holding her breath, or if the entire world around them was doing the same. For a moment, the breeze seemed to still in the trees, the sounds of the fête growing suddenly silent. She blinked rapidly, her eyes hot and prickling as she slowly edged to the front of the bench, her hands reaching out to cradle Ivan's face.

'Yes,' she whispered, her voice thick with emotion. 'A thousand times yes.'

As his face cracked into the widest smile, he slid the ring on her finger and pulled her close, his mouth claiming hers in a way she knew she would never in a dozen lifetimes grow weary of. And as he held her to him, she felt her chest rise and fall against his, her body fitting his as though they were handcrafted for each other.

'I love you,' he murmured, his breath tickling her ear and sending shivers down his spine. 'And I believe in us—in the family we will become.'

'I love you,' she echoed softly. Reverently.

Three simple words that held myriad promises.

'Whatever life looks like in the future,' he told her solemnly, taking her face in his hands and staring deep into her eyes as though he could see through to her very soul, 'we'll face it together, won't we?'

'Together,' she agreed, a sincere vow that held every bit of promise she would ever have. 'Now and forever.'

And as his arms enveloped Ruby in an embrace that felt like the closing of a circle, the final suturing of a wound that had been open and aching for years, her response was every bit as fervent. Winding her arms around his neck, she allowed him to pull her close, then moved herself closer still. The village fête was still going on in the distance—its laughter, its music, its clattering games—fading into a distant hum as their focus narrowed to each other.

'Ruby,' Ivan murmured, his voice a low rumble against her ear.

She tilted her head back, gazing into his eyes, those deep pools of blue that had once seemed inscrutable but now overflowed with emotion until finally, *finally*, his lips met hers in a kiss that was more than just a mere meeting of lips. It was a promise. A vow. A pledge of shared tomorrows. Passionate and tender all at once, it was a kiss that spoke of battles fought and won, of fears overcome, and of a future ripe with possibility.

He might have kissed her for a lifetime—he might have kissed for two—all Ruby knew was she lost in a moment that she never wanted to end. And when they did reluctantly pull apart, their faces remaining close, and their breath still mingling, Ivan tenderly brushed a lock of hair behind Ruby's ear, his touch reverent.

'Thank you, Ivan,' she breathed at last.

'What for?'

'For finally having the courage to let yourself love me.'

'You are easy to love, Ruby Channing,' he assured her. 'But it is me who should thank you for being my beacon, and my hope. You guided me to the light when I didn't even realize I was lost in the darkness.'

And as they stood there, on the periphery of the village yet still a part of it, Ruby knew that together they would build not just a family, but a sanctuary—a haven of love, understanding, and unwavering support.

Their journey was just beginning, and Ruby knew she couldn't wait to find out where it would lead them. Because as long as Ivan was by her side, she was no longer living in a bubble, too afraid to enter the world outside Little Meadwood.

In fact, she was finally ready to face anything.

* * * * *

If you enjoyed this story,
check out these other great reads from
Charlotte Hawkes

Trauma Doc to Redeem the Rebel
Neurosurgeon, Single Dad… Husband?
His Cinderella Houseguest
Shock Baby for the Doctor

All available now!